CAN'T CA

Can't Catch Me
and other twice-told tales

MICHAEL CADNUM

TACHYON PUBLICATIONS · SAN FRANCISCO

Can't Catch Me and Other Twice-Told Tales

Interior design & composition by John D. Berry
The typeface is Garamond Premier Pro

Tachyon Publications
1459 18th Street #139
San Francisco, ca 94107
(415) 285-5615
www.tachyonpublications.com

Series Editor: Jacob Weisman

ISBN 10: 1-892391-33-3
ISBN 13: 978-1-892391-33-3

Printed in the United States of America
by the Maple-Vail Manufacturing Group

First Edition: 2006

9 8 7 6 5 4 3 2 1

for Sherina

One raven
one raven
and the lake

CONTENTS

CAN'T CATCH ME

Bear it Away

after "Goldilocks and the Three Bears"

I NEVER LIKED THE WOODLAND, even in my youth, but the forest here was not one of your lowly hoar-wilds, all crag and moss.

It was really very pleasant, a happy mix of pinecones and little red ants, dock and nettles. You wouldn't want to muss your skirt, going on a picnic in the cockle burrs. But it was a nice enough wood, little yellow flowers when the snow melted, and mushrooms shaped like willies. Some of our more prominent watercolorists traveled here to set up their easels, and botanists collected herbs along the streams.

A maiden could go berry picking with the silversmith's son, or slip off to meet the young professor from down-valley, and if she ran across a bear it would be one of the old traditional bears, little eyes, big rumps, snuffling the air, trying to see if you were trouble or something to eat. If a bear said anything at all it was in antique bear-tongue, not much to it, really, just good-bye or go away, all a bear needed to know.

From time to time a typical bear fracas broke out. A sow bear killed a miller down by the well, for example, when he stepped on a cub, it being night and the miller having lost his spectacles in the inn. The she-bear threw him over her shoulder and left him by the quarrymen's privy quite a boneless puddle. But what did we expect?

It was reassuring, in a way, having bears to worry about. Kids afraid of the dark were easier to quiet down. A sudden gust or a scuttling acorn on the roof and mom and dad would roll their eyes and whisper, "A bear looking for children who won't eat their cabbage!"

Gentlemen of rude humor would disguise a burp by muttering, "Must've been a bear, growling in the glade," and if things got boring on a long summer's day, the villagers would unpen the hounds, run down a granddad bruin, and pen the bear in a sandpit.

It was sport, all fair play, it seemed, joy under a summer's eve. Bets would flow hand to hand on the question which would expire first, bear or dog. Life was simple.

Mosquitoes and holidays, ale and bearskins.

But it changed.

Some people say it was better nutrition, trout multiplying as the rivers ran clear. The weather changed, the magnetic poles shifted – we all had our theories. I don't know how, but it happened. One day we had dumb bears rolling logs to gobble worms, and the next we had bears in the vicarage library. They were wood-bears, still, and kept off to themselves, when they weren't stocking up on rhyming dictionaries. But a revolution was underway.

It could be overlooked for a while. Bears still slept half the year and they still had trouble seeing. But when a boar-bear lumbered into the fletcher's wife one afternoon and offered effusive apologies for treading on her toe, we all knew something profound had happened to bear nature. The bears rushed her to the surgeon and stood around waiting for news of her recovery.

Mrs. Fletcher regained her health and sanity, until she stepped out a week later to take some medicinal sun. A bear made-way from the midden, dainty-like, a she-bear, and said, "I hope I see you well."

Which simple remark killed the fletcher's dame that moment — she died of the shock.

Many of us understood exactly. I didn't mind a bit of sass from a blue jay or the tinsmith's mutt, but I did think that this was more than mortal humans need endure, a curtsy from a bear wearing a bonnet.

Myself, I was blonde, and if the glazier liked the look of me as well as the joiner, why, let them all have an eyeful, was how I always felt. I was charitable with my smiles, but when a bear asked how I was on this finest of mornings, and held the post office door open for me, I hurried right past and never said a word.

A long era of tranquility was underway, bears writing essays, offering opinions on the likelihood of rain, bears making excellent neighbors. And most humans liked this, an age of peace. But I never got use to bears reading haiku, bears laughing at our human jokes. Months went by, entire seasons, and a bear never ate a single human. Not one.

There was bear-laughter and bear-song, noon and night.

I had a plan.

I WANTED A HUNTER, one of those always just in time to drill a musket shot through a wolf's lights. And if he was fine of leg and loin, I wouldn't mind parting the bracken a bit with such a man, not being quite so young as I had been, and looking for the right sort to share my winter nights. Although this was not the point-entire. I wanted to teach the bears why they shouldn't weave rugs and write plays, and give them a lesson they'd never forget.

I wanted to teach them to keep their bear-talk to themselves. And if the cottage-dwelling men were too weak-kneed to educate the bears, I'd find myself a red-jacketed crack shot and make him mine.

And so I did. He was a square-jawed elk-hunter from the vale to the east. His red jacket was sappy-brown along the sleeves, and he smelled of brandy, but he showed me how he double-powdered both barrels and blew twin holes in my mum's quilt hanging out to dry — and he paid gold florins for a new one.

He was perfect.

I recall that early morning well, how I tickled him awake. I tugged him from the bed, red-cheeked, unshaven. I remember the dawn as if it were a week ago, although these days I'm the only one alive who can sing the words to a single bear madrigal. I led my hunter to the woods, mist in the tulips, wood smoke in the thatch. I filled him with my scheme, and before I let him yea-or-nay, I kissed him wide awake, and said, "Follow me."

Bears are fond of walking — or they were, our wise bears used to be. They walked, they slept. Peripatetic brethren, as the priest would say, they were always cooking their oats, howling when the porridge scalded, and using the excuse for another ramble, up one trail and down the next. My hunter and I spied a family, dad, mum, and wee one. They ambled off, blinking in the sunlight, happy as cows to be out in the grass, the little one hopping, rabbit-like.

"Stay here," I whispered to my gunner.

I hid behind a berry bush. I waited, and when the family vanished up the trail, I scurried into the cottage.

I violated their breakfast bowls, hot and cold, and made sure they would see the mess when they returned to the table. Spoon and finger, I tasted, scooped, and splattered. (It was delicious – just the right amount of honey.) I did what I could with the furniture, the chairs and settles too stout for the likes of me to break. All I could manage was a high chair in the corner, one the bear-lad must have just outgrown.

I broke that into kindling, and left it sowed around the nook. I took myself upstairs. I flung wide the shutters so Redcoat would hear me shriek when the time came, and I settled myself in the largest of the three beds. This mattress was packed with straw so coarse it was like sprawling in a thicket.

So I tried the middle bed, just my size, but it was so cratered by the weight of Mistress Griz that I climbed up and down the bedding, clinging to the edges.

Finally I escaped the bed and found the laddie's bunk, and slept. Why did you fall asleep, moon-calf, I would demand of myself in years to come. And I have no retort. No clever answer to myself. I lay, I slept. Not one to stoop to excuses, but mayhap the hunter's nip, that brandy wine he said was courage, overdid my wakefulness. "Just a taste," he had said, tasting some himself.

I never heard them on their way. When the three rambled back into the cottage, I had no inkling they were home, peering at their porridge, aghast at the broken high chair, nosing the air. Or perhaps I had a hint of what was happening, in one part of my mind.

Step by step, they ascended to the bedroom. The oak door

creaked. Their heavy steps were slow, the floorboards groaning. Only then did I hear them, words as clear as any tinker's. "What's this – my pillow all mussed," said the father.

"And here, my mattress half-in, half-out," said Mum-bear, nearsighted, nose to her bed. "And me, and me!" cried the pup-bruin. "My bed too!" he cried.

I am now the only one in the land who knows, how like to our own speech it was, this language, this bear-tongue. "Mine too," he stammered, "and she is still – still here!"

I didn't have to feign my horror, yelling from the window, tangled in a sheet, screaming, bellowing. I called out, "What are you waiting for?" But my huntsman was lying in plain sight, sound asleep in the green grass, sunlight gleaming off his gun.

"She's here, she's here!" cried the cub. Both parents trying to make me out, blinking in the bright morning light through the open window.

I ran home.

In my haste, I soaked my skirts in the ford, dragged them in the thistles, muddied them and tore them, all the way to hearth and safety. I was scolded by my mum, and I sobbed into the shot-rent quilt, swearing virtue, good deeds, and chastity to God.

I kept my visit secret.

And a perfect secret it was, too. Except.

Except that the silence fell.

No ursine gardeners peddled roots from door to door. No kindly bear held the pasture gate to let a goodwife pass. No bear song drifted from the meadow. Nine days later a pigeon-hunter accidentally uncovered the powder horn, one weather-glazed hunter's boot, and one sap-stained quarter of a jacket.

"A mishap," said the magistrate, eyeing the tooth marks in the shoulder of the scrap. "A lamentable misadventure," he added, with sadness. "And a deep mystery, as well."

Anyone could see the nature of the hunter's sudden end, but the sheriff said it was beyond us all, what might have taken place. Because the bears were loved, and loved in return, in their bluff, like-human way.

But all the bears had vanished. Their cottages stood dark. No one knew what caused this blight, or where the speaking grizzlies repaired to, why they left our woods.

No one except myself.

The last time I saw a bear beside a creek, not a fortnight past, she stood on her two hind paws and listened while I bid her a good evening. "And good health to you," I said.

She turned away, and left me alone, the stream beside me running like a song.

Only I know, and I keep it to myself. But I see too clearly what happened. I know exactly how the huntsman leaped to his feet, face red with sleep and drink. I see too well in the eye of my mind how the Redcoat brandished his double-shotted gun.

I see him drawing aim upon the cub, and in my waking dream I see what a bear can eat for breakfast, when she has to on a sunny morn.

Can't Catch Me

after "The Gingerbread Man"

WHAT IT WAS WAS HOT.

Hot is fine if you want to get from being so much goop, and turn into something with a little structural integrity, but when you have what it takes you don't need hot anymore.

People say, Hey, Hot is sacred. And I say sure, you give Hot its due. I don't go around writing my name on ovens with Day-Glo paint, and I don't think you should encourage people to say Hot is nothing. But if you honestly expect me to spend any time at all visiting stoves and ovens and kitchens because some people think that the whole place would be nothing without a stove in the first place, I say you can forget all of that sanctimonious stove cant. I have no use for it.

So, I get out of the stove and the first thing you notice is: it's not hot.

Nobody talks about this. Parents, all they think about is the wood, the ashes, the ventilator, all they think about is keeping the heat. They never think to let you know what it's going to be like. They want you in the stove. That's what they want. You'd burn up in there, sure, but parents want you in the stove. "Keep him in the box," they think, "and we'll know where he is at night." It could kill you, but they know where you are.

So I'm out. I'm cold.

It was a shock, I can tell you, and I think I might have been a little bit more prepared, but I know everyone says that Mom and Dad should have done a better job, and I get tired of people blaming someone else for their problems. It's cheap, it's easy. I found out it was cold, I survived. But I could have been given a hint or two or a few clues. I could have been taken out for a little bit now and then to see what it was like. Because the truth is that when I got out it was on the run. I had been in there way too long. I was fast because I knew they wanted me hot so long I'd have ashes for britches. Parents do that. "So what he's a charcoal colored crisp, he's my boy." I ran.

And you wouldn't believe the noise. You'd think nobody had ever run in the history of kitchens. My mother wailing, "My boy is running." And then she couldn't even finish the thought, practically gagging on the words. "My boy is running — " and she coughed out the word "away!" Tears, moaning, grabbing at her heart. I was cold, I was running. My father is after me, and you know how old guys are. They like to prove they're in shape and they like old guys who can wrestle a hog or toss a stack of hay down to another guy who really ought to be up there forking the load so the old guy won't die of a heart attack. But old guys like to show they aren't old and end up slipping on a great swath of goose guano, which is what my father did.

I wasn't all that happy to hear him go down, and I even looked back to see if he was at least not going to need one of those devices you see on really messed up old guys, those things made out of straps, like a cage for the knee. But then I see my father is up, not because he's in physical condition for this kind of thing, but because the goose guano is a little thick around the puddles and he has some on his face. And he's hollering. He can't run but he can holler. He has a holler that scares roosters. So I really start to run, and then I see the neighbors.

We all have neighbors. I don't care who you are, you have neighbors. Maybe far away and you never see them except when their house floats down the river with one of them stuck on it yelling but you know them when you see them. Those are mine you think. My neighbors.

Well, here come the neighbors. Now you have put up with Mom and Dad. You know they are pathetic but if they are so totally dead-bone thoroughly pathetic that doesn't make you look so good, either. So you allow that maybe your parents, at one time, and maybe still for maybe one second a month, have a little dignity or sense, or at least know how to tell a fry pan from a cowpie, if it's not too dark. But you don't have to extend such broad-mindedness to neighbors, and let me say that these people would have taken a great deal of liberal open-mindedness and allowances for all kinds of foibles and defects and still come up wanting, because these neighbors were barbarians, big, slow, mean, and hairy. Except one was bald. And they weren't even that slow.

These guys don't care about me. My mother is a demented maniac but at least she had a set of assumptions about where I was and where I was going to be that make you at least understand why she's upset. And my Dad, having green stuff on his face and practically in his mouth, you can really understand he's got a lot of responsibility and pride and self-image on the line right there and then if he doesn't pick those feet up and put them down pretty successfully.

But the neighbors, they basically just want to tear into me.

That's the only way I can put it. They would just take a big chunk right out of me, and swallow it whole. They never heard of me, practically, until that very minute, but they start baying after me just like they had every right in the world. And one of the neighbors could run.

As fast as I was, I decided that my best bet was to play a little psychology and find one of those high places you see in roads, where the ruts have made a little mountain, sometimes so high it scrapes an axle. And I stand up there and I say that famous line.

Don't make me repeat it, it was all I could think of at the time. I'll say it once here, for just the sake of accuracy and not because I think it was the most brilliant thing ever said or anything like that, but let me tell you it was easily a match for anything coming out of the faces of my Dad or the neighbors.

I said the famous run and run line, as fast as you can, and then I decided I will adopt a little sobriquet, give myself a nom de run, as it were, and I said "I'm the Gingerbread Man," but I really said it more or less to myself. I didn't think anyone was listening. It was just one of those things you end up being famous for and it's on T-shirts and people say did you really and you have to admit to it: that's what I said. And then one of the neighbors, a really big one, and hairy, was really running. This guy was a fast farmer.

He had a pitchfork, and where I come from these are by no consideration petite. These are big wagon-load-size wooden fences attached to a pole, except it's not a fence, it's a row of big wooden spikes. And this guy is getting ready to throw this fork so if he forgets how to move his feet in the next second or two, which is pretty possible judging from the look in his eye which is, to be charitable, stupid, then the fork will arc through the air and nail me where I am and that will be the end of me.

Which is how I looked at it. I took this very personally. When someone is about to turn me into so much flour and spice I don't think about his uneven education or how his brothers probably are as bad off as he is and he doesn't know any better. I saw this big projectile, this birch wood pitchfork, leave this guy's arm and soar up high, and reach its apex, and what did I do?

Some people think that there is pride, and then over here, at the red end of the spectrum, you've got hubris. Pride is a problem, but we have to have it. Otherwise, we'd all go around looking like our neighbors. No pride equals no personal upkeep. But hubris is when you really ask for it. When you really think that nothing bad can ever happen to you because the Stove made you especially for a key purpose and nothing can ever hurt you.

What I did wasn't quite that bad, but it was close, I admit. With the big, knobby fork glittering in the light and coming down with an ugly quiet noise, not a whoosh, more of a whistle, I stopped. I put my hands on my hips. And I gave my speech a second time.

It was this version, when I had it all made up already, which I think was the one they heard and remembered. This was the speech that got to be famous. It was the very same one as the first one I ever said, no matter what some people might say. Let me admit here that I was scared. I was sure I was about to be crushed by a tine as big as a wagon tongue.

And let me add, to be frank, when that fork landed in advance of where I stood, and where I would have been standing if I hadn't stopped and delivered what some people eventually called my Taunt, well, maybe I did give just a passing thought to the idea that maybe Stove was looking after me for just that instant. So then I really ran, and not just the sprint that I had already mastered, but a new method of transport altogether, more of a bounding than running, and I needed it because the pitchfork neighbor was bearing down on me for no reason at all except that he had forgotten the rest of the world existed and forgotten who he was and where he lived. As far as he knew he had always been running after me and there was nothing more to life than me and him and pretty soon there would be only him.

Many people are like that. Just knowing there is someone else running along makes them want to start throwing things. So I turned my head in the middle of my bounds and there was Pitchfork Neighbor, developing a little bound of his own, and getting closer, too. And so what did I do?

Well, I gave the speech again. I got off my speech, and it went pretty well, a little breathy and under-projected but not too bad under the circumstances. And the Pitchfork Neighbor had me. There was riparian mud underfoot, the black stuff, and bounding was a distinctly poor choice because directly in front of me was water. The river here is not much. The current is slow and you might see a flood once every four or five years, otherwise this is not the sort of river to inspire song. Pitchfork Neighbor is not one to flinch at a little mud: he dived, he had me in his right hand, and he was squeezing.

By now I had been through some experience, and I was able to reflect upon the nature of the nuclear family, the way it loves you until it kills you, and then the nature of the rest of the world, how it just goes right ahead and kills you without bothering with any sort of emotional bonding. I see how relatively puny I am, being a construct of flour and sugar, and how both malleable and detachable my body parts are.

I left a finger in each one of Pitchfork Neighbor's eyes, debarked his grip without a further recitation of my speech, and ran up the river through reeds and algae, in great danger of losing my structural format altogether, when what should come slinking along the reeds but an unattractive creature, one of our river foxes, a smart but demoralized breed of animal, overly trained in one of those professions that fade but never quite go away. You hear a lot of bad things about river foxes, but they are still an animal you want to emulate if you want to be a liar.

The late morning sun glittered on the river. The sky was empty blue. There were footsteps, and cries, reeds snapping, mud slopping. A voice bellowed, "There he is!"

The fox regarded me.

The fox and I worked out an arrangement whereby he would carry me on his back across the river, at a point which, inconveniently, the river was at its widest. It was all he could do to keep from drowning. He splashed, struggled, so out of shape he could hardly enunciate words without shipping water into his snout, plus I think we had a substance abuse problem here. This was a sad circumstance, a fox lacking pride. Anyway, by now everyone knows how he got me on his head, and then on his snout, and then how he ate me with a snap.

This is true. I got eaten.

Everybody loves this part of the story. Youthful insouciance gets a hard and terminal lesson in hubris. But ginger and foxes don't agree. It happens. Try giving aspirin to a cat. It kills them. So I have some digestive juice to contend with. At least it's not an oven. It's not heat.

Compared with the family hearth and home, fox vomit is nothing. And by the time the fox is heaving on the other shore, what's left of me is enough to run faster than ever.

Well, sort of run. And my career begins. Nothing special, but you've heard of me. I stay out of the water, and out of the kitchen.

It's not the winners who write history, it's the neighbors.

Hungry

[1]

THE TAXI DROPPED ME OFF at the dock in a heavy mist, the ebbing tide and the marina's boat slips all a dim presence through the wet gray.

"Are you sure this where you want me to leave you?" asked the driver, a pleasant blonde who had told me she was about to take a break for supper. And I was tempted, realizing that I was not at all sure what I was doing. However, I was altogether certain that I did not like this place.

"It's not safe," added the driver.

I was keenly aware of how easily a life could be lost. My wife of ten years had died the previous winter of a rare, previously unheard-of malady associated with global warming, toxic mold spores causing a profound sleeping sickness, and an absolute departure from life. I had kept busy in the lab, but after a year of bereavement Esther's loss was still the central and enduring fact of my days and nights.

Now, feeling that I was about to be stranded in the middle of a foggy, unknown place, I squared my shoulders, and thanked the taxi driver warmly. When in doubt, I had always directed myself, act like you know what you are doing.

"Right down the coast about a mile and a half," the driver continued, pointing with her forefinger without removing her hand from the wheel, "is where they found one of the bodies."

During the drive, prompted by her curiosity, I had admitted that I was a scientist. She had been an overflowing source of rumors regarding the notorious series of local deaths, bodies found along the coast attributed variously to sea monsters, human attackers, sharks. Each had been slashed, nearly in two, from throat to pelvis. "Opened right up," as she had put it, "like books."

The dead included a financial consultant, a psychiatrist, and a television producer. "And their insides were eaten," she had added with a certain stony relish.

I gave the cabdriver a wave, and watched as the gloaming swallowed the Crown Victoria's brake lights. She had seemed nervous but determined, one dispatcher's call away from ending up like the high-profile victims, flung like a used paperback along the Central Coast.

A police car appeared out of the fog, and slowed as its inhabitants studied me. It was one of those unmarked vehicles, lime-green, with California state plates. The passenger window rolled down and a heavily-jacketed policewoman asked me if I needed help.

What she really wanted to know, I imagined, was whether or not I was the sort of person who killed and ate people.

I told her, "I'm waiting for a boat."

She looked me up and down as I tried to appear both harmless and capable of defending myself.

"Be careful," she said at last.

They circled back to watch me again, either offering me their protective attention or still suspicious. I actually missed the police as they drove off.

Everyone was anxious about something. In addition to the usual background noise of crime and Middle Eastern war, inexplicable animals had been showing up where they had been thought eradicated, or where they didn't belong at all.

A timber wolf had been trapped in a building on San Francisco's Montgomery Street, and Big Foot had reportedly killed two deer poachers in the Trinity Alps. No reliable observer really believed the violence had been caused by the legendary Sasquatch, but my friends at Fish and Game had shown me the crime scene photos, and I had no explanation for the brutality.

A few tentative experts opined that excessive carbon dioxide in the air was driving lost species out of hiding. National Geographic had sent a team to examine a supposed centaur in Macedonia. There were stories of elf-sized humans in Indonesia and a band of Cyclops near the Black Sea.

Sometimes fog offers a sense of quiet serenity. But not on this mid-January afternoon — not for me. Yachts in the mooring slips along the Oxnard marina kept their identities well hidden under canvas tarps and plastic sheets, the wintery weather closing in as the day ran out of strength, and only the throaty rumble of an engine somewhere off beyond the Ventura County coastline gave me any indication of promise.

When the power-yacht chugged into sight, and eased into place against the wharf pads I stepped forward eagerly, but there was no welcome from the vessel, only an air of furtive quiet.

I could not shake the sensation of being carefully observed by the occupants of the handsome vessel, and I did a hurried inventory of my person — blue Gor-Tex jacket, backpack, hiking boots — as though to verify to myself, at least, that I presented an innocent appearance.

I had not yet met Webster's new wife, and was not sure what I would make of her. Without any particular reason, I had felt uncharacteristically shy about meeting her. Nonetheless, I was relieved when someone approached the yacht's rail and a woman's voice called, "You must be Dr. Ford."

I admitted as much with a tone of heartfelt relief, and insisted that she call me Matthew.

"I am Anaclette Brentwood." She offered me a mittened hand, helping me into the yacht.

I must have expected Webster to greet me on the yacht as well. She answered my unvoiced question, explaining, "My husband awaits us on the island."

She was heavily garbed in a cape, with its hood thrown back, appropriate protection against the damp. She was dark-haired, taller than I had expected. She gave me a searching look, both curious and friendly. Her eyes were gray, and she looked into my gaze longer than was necessary. The glance she gave me was surprising, and it stirred something in me that I felt was both inappropriate and exceedingly pleasant.

"What runs away," she asked, "only to catch up with us?"

I thought I had not understood her.

She stepped closer, and repeated her query as the yacht churned the water, preparing to head seaward.

I glanced around at the out-coursing swells with some surprise at being asked a riddle by this beautifully unnerving woman.

Our surroundings offered me a clue.

"The tide!" I said with a laugh.

She smiled.

With scarcely a moment's small talk, Mrs. Brentwood was giving me what could only be called another long and decidedly seductive look.

"Are you hungry?" she asked.

I was surprisingly without appetite.

"No, thanks."

"Sometimes I am so very hungry," she said, as though coyly confessing a private failing. The sexual implication was not lost on me. "But you will certainly want a hot drink," she added.

It was a statement, and one with which I could agree gratefully.

"I'll prepare one for you," she said.

She had a remarkable way of speaking, choosing her words carefully in a low, almost commanding voice. I had never met a woman like her, and if I possessed a clearer sense of my own emotions I would have recognized that I was close to falling instantly in love with the wife of my former teacher.

I knew little about her, except that, according to rumor, she was foreign-born and that he had met her on his travels. Her accent was indeed exotic, but I could not place it.

Anaclette excused herself and went below.

The seacraft wasted no time in making way quickly from the ghostly outlines of masts and prows, and past the faint demarcation of the breakwater.

Soon we outraced the ebbing tide and cut a wake outward, toward the distant Channel Islands.

[2]

AS ANACLETTE RETURNED to press a warm mug into my hands — coffee laced with scotch and fortified with brown sugar, by the taste of it — a Coast Guard cutter approached through the mist.

A searchlight speared the wet, and played across the deck. I didn't mind at all, satisfied that the authorities were busy protecting us. The yacht slowed, the deck sawing unevenly under my feet and I had to take great care not to spill my coffee.

An amplified voice from the cutter asked us to identify our vessel, and our pilot responded with our name and our destination — Abalone Harbor, San Pedro Island.

The cutter was a vague hulk through the fog, and the searchlight illuminated the water droplets in the air until they glittered, spinning and surging like microscopic snow. The bright light swept us, the light beam heavy, like a physical weight. I had to close my eyes against the glare.

Anaclette sighed with relief as the cutter's amplified voice wished us a safe arrival, the light was turned off, and the cutter altered her course.

Our yacht returned again to full power. The mug of spiked coffee was welcome against the chill, and it brought back memories of my fieldwork with Webster Brentwood, studying the tule elk of the Point Reyes herds, rising before dawn on chilly mornings to watch the young bulls bugle plaintively, and fight, sometimes, crashing their antlers together with surprising impact.

"You will have many questions," Anaclette was saying.

I agreed that I probably would have more than a few questions, taking refuge in understatement. "Webster hasn't hatched a few dinosaurs out there on the island, has he?" I asked jokingly.

"If only it were something so easy, Matthew," she responded, raising her voice over the rumble of the engine. "Webster is looking forward to seeing you. You know how he loves to explain what he has done."

"He often has a good deal to explain," I said with a laugh.

"He is better at explanations, perhaps," she said, "than he is at answers. He is in trouble."

I knew the man well, and, in a sense, I had outgrown him.

Webster Brentwood had begun his honored career by introducing wolves into landscapes where they had been long ago run out of existence. He had developed ways of managing populations of elk and bison, using species-specific birth control chemicals to control successful populations.

But sometimes he made a mistake, like the unannounced introduction of a grizzly bear into the Santa Cruz mountains. Only his quick work with a heavy-caliber rifle had saved a cabin dwelling family from being slaughtered by the large, ill-humored carnivore he had himself raised as a cub.

Some of his colleagues whispered that Webster did not simply reintroduce displaced species – he reconstituted them, tickling DNA into new configurations, reawaking long-lost nene geese and dire wolves from protein fibers in various natural history museums. One otherwise sober associate of mine had asserted that Webster Brentwood hoped to bring the saber-toothed tiger into modern times, but I had merely brushed the suggestion aside.

Now, as the yacht sped into the darkness, I looked forward to seeing my erstwhile mentor, but I was worried about him, too. I had to hang onto the rail to stay upright and the vessel cut through the slow, winter swells. The *Anaclette Mariposa* was powered by a heavy diesel engine, and piloted by a heavyset man well protected by a sweater and watch cap, and visible through the windowed door to the cabin.

Anaclette leaned out over the taffrail, eyeing the wake for signs of – what, I wondered? The Coast Guard cutter's light probed the fog, increasingly far away. If any other craft followed us, she was lost in the thick twilight.

Once my eyes adjusted to the running lights, I was able to see well enough. I wandered the vessel, taking note of the fire extinguisher, the No Smoking sign, and the flare gun secure behind glass.

An ax gleamed above the rail along steps down into what I gathered were sleeping berths, and if I had to guess the contents of a sturdy wooden case set against the bulkhead I would have imagined shotguns, several of them, although why a boat owner would store firearms on a yacht, and face the routine of oiling the weapons and checking their loads against the salt air, I could not imagine.

It is not very easy to grope your way along a yacht moving at twenty knots, salt-flavored mist and ocean spray making everything even wetter. I approached the pilot's cabin with care.

There beside the handle-spoked wheel of the helm was a shotgun, upright and secure, like the firearm carried by any number of squad cars. The pilot sensed my presence. He turned and gave me a preoccupied smile through the salt-glazed glass, and then he turned again to watch the beam of light from our prow as it swept the mist, gilding the spuming whitecaps and the occasional climbing wings of a seabird.

Surely some people considered it a sport to empty chum into the swells and use a pump-gun on the sharks that show up to have lunch, but when I saw an additional firearm, an automatic in a holster set high on Anaclette's hip, beneath her mantle, I got the impression of a two-person crew that was ready to handle trouble. I groped aft through the mist, realizing that this pleasure yacht would have been a graceful and welcoming vessel, under entirely different circumstances.

Anaclette came toward me, having no trouble walking forward on the wet, heaving teakwood deck. "We'll be another hour, at least," she said apologetically. "San Pedro is the most remote of all the Channel Islands."

My former professor had sent me a letter, with the neatly inked request at the bottom, "Burn this after you've committed it."

To memory, he meant, but it was just like Webster Brentwood's clipped, direct style, and it was just like me, the former graduate school darling of the distinguished scientist, to follow his instructions exactly, using three matches to make sure the heavy rag paper caught fire and flamed entirely to ash.

What had impressed me most about the letter, which was an enigmatic but cordial welcome to his island estate "as soon as possible," had been the additional query, "Do you still know how to use a dart gun?"

It was true that I could fire an accurate dose of PCP at forty meters – not that easy to do. But the letter had explained nothing. When a man of Webster Brentwood's magnetism writes "I need your help," you postpone the committee meetings and lunch with your agent and grab your shaving kit and toothbrush.

"Our house is secure," said Anaclette, leaning beside me as I watched the ocean streak past all but invisibly in the darkness.

"Secure against what?"

"Matthew, I can't talk about such a thing myself."

I took her choice of words seriously. Such a thing.

Perhaps realizing that she had already said too much, she added, "San Pedro is the only Channel Island with springwater. Anacapa Island doesn't have it, and even Santa Catalina is naturally dry."

Perhaps she was hoping I could be put off with such travelogue tidbits. She was very nearly right. San Pedro Island was owned by the State of California, but a Maybeck-designed house there and all the sixty square miles of land were leased to Stanford University for ecological research.

Wild boar had been introduced into the rocky canyons in the 1920s as sporting creatures, and the voracious animals had rooted and tusked the island's few native oak trees nearly out of existence. State game marksmen had long since put the last of these boars onto menus of exclusive restaurants in Los Angeles, and the island had been largely restored to its primordial, if rugged, condition.

"Something's gone wrong, hasn't it?" I asked.

Perhaps I expected her to offer a smiling, No, of course not.

Instead she looked away.

"You know how Webster is," she said. "He invites what should be left uninvited, and then what is he to do?"

The ocean isn't a clean, virgin expanse of water any longer. As we coursed our way west we struck litter, gasoline cans and plastic bottles spun past to join our wake. We struck other floating objects, too, the hull echoing with muffled but definite sounds of impact – drift logs, perhaps, or the tree-sized growths of giant kelp that forest the well-traveled channel.

Anaclette leaned out over the rail at the sound of the larger collisions. Night boating could be dangerous to craft and creatures alike – seals and whales had both been known to suffer injuries.

About an hour off the mainland the mist broke. A lingering veil of damp swept over us, and then the night sky was brilliant with stars.

Our destination loomed to the west, black hills cutting their silhouettes out of the night sky. I was happy to see the damp weather come to an end, but Anaclette unsnapped the strap of her holster, eyeing the constellations above.

Diesel fumes rose up around us as the yacht thundered, backing up, and at last nudging the wharf. I was eager to leap from the vessel, but Anaclette put a hand on my arm. "Wait for Rolando to give the all clear. It makes him feel better."

Rolando was not only a capable pilot, it seemed, but he was also a trusted security man. I tossed lines to him, and waited as he secured the vessel, and then stood waiting on the dock as he disappeared into the darkness, in the direction of a grand, dimly lit house in the distance. As he made his way across the dark lawn he tugged a handgun from inside his jacket, a heavyweight revolver, and he strode with firearm in one fist, flashlight in the other.

"It's OK for now," he said on his return.

"Did you check the roof?" insisted Anaclette.

"I checked everything, Mrs. Brentwood, as well as I could. But please be careful." He was matter-of-fact, but in my judgment, he sounded tense.

A voice in me, rational and none-too-brave, insisted that I wasn't setting foot on this island until someone explained all the precautions.

But I followed the two of them up a long line of stepping-stones, toward a large, elegant house handsomely displayed in the starlight. I looked upward to examine the lofty branches of a grandfather Monterey pine, easily the tallest tree nearby. No predator appeared on any of the branches, neither owl nor cat of any kind.

Anaclette turned back to beckon me.

"If she sees you," she said, "it is too late." Then she put her arm out to mine, giving me a gentle squeeze with her mitten — and an unmistakable caress. "But I won't let anything bad happen to you, Matthew."

Perhaps I am not the only person to notice that stepping-stones are rarely placed to suit my stride. These were too close together, and then too far apart by way of variation. I half stumbled over a weed, and I kicked a pinecone out of my way. This sloping lawn, and this stretch of once-beautiful garden, had been allowed to go wild.

This historical place was neglected.

Or abandoned.

I was concerned at the sight of Rolando heading back toward the yacht, hurrying along, flashlight in his hand. He made quick work of unfastening the lines and starting the yacht's big diesel engine.

Anaclette said, "Rolando is like all the others — he won't spend a night on the island."

[3]

I WAS DISMAYED at the appearance of my former teacher.

He leaned heavily on a stout blackthorn stick, and his features were creased with pain as he limped forward to greet me. But what troubled him was far worse than pain – my one-time adviser was haggard with some inner turmoil.

My first remark to him was, "Webster, you're hurt!"

"It's not so bad," he chuckled, giving me a one-armed hug. "It's just a minor scrape."

His welcome was hearty, and he gestured grandly, in that outsized manner for which he was famous, but I could see that much of his enthusiasm about the view from the terrace and the enormous kitchen was forced. I was surprised, too, at my own reaction to him.

I had once admired him, nearly to the point of devotion. But those feelings had died in me, and now I felt wary around the veteran scientist.

"I'll give you the grand tour some other time," he said, leading me into a room that was evidentially his study, a book-lined refuge with a fireplace glowing merrily against the island chill.

I already missed Anaclette's companionship, but she had vanished into the interior of the house.

Webster shut the door quietly but firmly, and twisted a lock. "It is so good to see you, Matthew," he said with a warm smile. "You've been on my mind constantly. We all miss Esther so much."

Esther had made a favorite dish of Webster's, sturgeon poached in dry sherry, early in our marriage, before my mentor left to live on the island. She had confided to me that she regarded Webster as a force of nature, but with no more sense of caution than a six-year-old.

She had told me further that he once made an awkward but

unmistakable play for her between the sturgeon and the chocolate cake, an event about which I had never confronted Webster, but which cooled my admiration for the scientist considerably. In recent years we had exchanged Christmas cards, and little else.

"Of course, I've always been fond of you," Webster was saying. "Everyone likes you, am I right? Animals, women, children. You are likeable."

I thanked him, aware that, for all his genuine friendship toward me, he was trying to flatter me into doing something I might not want to do.

When we were both seated in leather chairs, each with a glass of scotch, he said, "I can still stitch up a wound, without an analgesic, just a needle and a thread. It's a useful skill."

"Maybe you should see a doctor," I suggested.

He shrugged. "I have sent the staff back to the mainland, those that didn't quit, or — or have a bit of bad luck."

I would have enjoyed this room under other circumstances, its high ceiling with oak beams, its brilliant carpet. But I felt that a secret was constantly being whisked just out of my sight, and I had already guessed that an animal of some sort — perhaps some experimental or even fabulous creature — had escaped and gotten into mischief.

I kept my tone conversational, but I did not like the sound of this. "What sort of 'bad luck'?"

"You know how responsible I feel for people who work for me." His voice was hoarse, and he rubbed a hand over his eyes.

"Yes," I rejoined, "and I remember the time you wanted to take a gorilla on BART."

"Jessica was a very wise subject," Webster said, "and I wanted to see her confronting the ticket machines."

"And then," I continued, "there was the time I had to put three darts into that hyena."

"Well, I admit the hyena was a mistake."

"What made you think," I asked, "that you could keep one as a pet?"

He smiled thoughtfully, with, perhaps, a pang of nostalgia for earlier, easier challenges. "Hilda was a companion more than a pet."

"Is she still happy at the Zurich zoo?"

He sighed, shaking his head, I believed, not at the memory of his cackling, cat-and-dog-devouring companion, but at his current predicament. "The last I heard Hilda was in bliss."

"Webster, what have you done now?"

He shook off the question, as though he could not bring himself to address the subject directly. His guarded, deeply shaken frame of mind disturbed me.

"You remember the time I captured a dragon in Crete?"

"Yes, I helped you."

"An actual fire-breathing dragon," he continued dreamily, happy at the memory.

I remembered the little green lizard well. It kept the lab free of flies and ants with its long, red tongue, and then it was slightly injured when an assistant shut a door on its tail. The creature set the lab alight in an apparent fit of annoyance, and died in the three-alarm blaze that ensued.

"You could keep it in a shoebox," I said. "It was very small."

"But it breathed fire!"

"It ignited gastro-produced methane," I said, "with a small electric charge, like a cross between an electric eel and a cigarette lighter."

"But," he said, leaning forward and spilling some of his scotch, "Matthew, it proved the old myths of fiery dragons were essentially true."

"True in a way," I admitted.

Webster spilled more of his whiskey in his eagerness to share a secret with me. "What if a team captured a truly well-known supposedly mythical creature and I secured this fabulous beast here on this island for study."

This did indeed sound very interesting. "You found a unicorn?"

We had speculated on the existence of such a beast during my days as a research assistant. Now he crinkled his nose, and gave a dismissive shrug. "What would a unicorn have to say to us? A horse with a horn growing out of its head – what kind of insight could it offer?"

"You got your hands on a centaur," I said, "or maybe a satyr?"

"Those choices are in any event much more interesting," he responded, "you have to agree. Chiron the wise horse-man would be a worthy subject, and so would the Great God Pan. I would love to see you interviewing Pan, Matthew. What would you ask him, I wonder."

I wonder too, I thought dryly. I had a sinking feeling, and I wondered what I had ever admired in this starry-eyed megalomaniac.

"What if I had this wonderful, wise being shipped here," Webster continued, "and sheltered safely, far from harm. A creature of, let us say, legendary wisdom."

"What have you got here, Webster?"

He ignored my question, tugging open a drawer in the large drum table beside him and withdrawing a very large, rubberized flashlight. "Did you bring any ketamine?"

"PCP and ketamine aren't the animal tranquilizers of choice anymore," I said. "Phazadine is quicker and safer."

And, I thought, I ought to use a few centiliters of the stuff on you.

"I tried to hit her with a needle," Webster said, tugging on a jacket and struggling with the zipper, "but she was too quick. Besides, I can't bring myself to hurt her, not even that little bit."

A sound reached us from outside, a creaking of tree limbs. This was followed by a distant whisper, wings, I thought, beating through the night sky.

"Oh, yes," breathed Webster, gazing upward toward the noise. "She can fly far and well. Matthew, I don't want you to overreact to what I am about to say — I think she has done harm."

"What sort of harm?"

He looked away, into the fire. He was near tears. "Matthew, I think that it is possible — just remotely possible — that she has killed people."

[4]

"YOU'LL UNDERSTAND EVERYTHING as soon as you see her," said Webster, spearing the darkness with his flashlight beam.

I doubted that this would prove to be the case, but I humored my one-time teacher, following him along a muddy trail.

I carried what looked like a .22 caliber rifle, a Pneu-dart model 196 tranquilizer gun, while Webster had thrust a massive nickel-plated revolver into his pants — the kind you might see a

Highway Patrol officer using to stop a truck.

"But whatever happens," said Webster, "don't talk to her."

I was mystified and irritated beyond words.

"You start by talking to them," he added, "and pretty soon you're even more lost than they are."

We cautiously approached what looked like a child's play structure, climbing bars that had suffered a devastating calamity. As Webster's flashlight beam played over the bent and deformed ironwork I realized that I was looking at the remains of what had been a very sturdy cage. A force had wrenched open the iron structure, and the inhabitant had evidently escaped.

A pair of shackles, the circlets gleaming in the moonlight, waited like twin, living things, dangling from a nearby post.

"She'll be back," said Webster, with a mix of reverence and regret. "She likes to perch on that eucalyptus." He indicated a tall, weathered column, all that was left of a nonnative tree, its growth snapped off by a long-forgotten storm.

I still had no clear idea what beast or chimerical creature Webster believed he had caught, but by now I had heard far more than enough.

I wished I had joined Rolando in chugging eastward across the cold waters, as far as possible from this island, but I was also very much afraid that Webster had at last committed a fatal misjudgment, and that it was my responsibility to put an end to his blunder.

"There she is!" hissed Webster, seizing my arm.

But it was only an owl, gliding silently over the naked spine of the tree, a barn owl, banking its wings, skimming the hillside.

Did we wait for an hour, or longer?

The time wore down what little patience I had left, but I had been trained to wait beside salt licks and watering holes on every major continent. I slipped into my pose of alert stillness, inwardly seething but outwardly calm.

"I think I hear her," said Webster at last, but neither of us expected to see any marvel circling above us.

And we did not, only a gull awake in the darkness, winging along in the increasing light of the moon.

I did not ask Webster what made him believe that his monster – whatever she might be – was a killer. I had taken in enough tales of sundered corpses to accept any violent explanation of events. I further believed that – whether because of his years of intellectual strain, or long isolation on this island – the respected scientist Webster Brentwood was no longer of sound mind.

Webster tugged at my sleeve.

He pointed skyward, his finger trembling.

I should have asked what we were going to do once we dropped her. A pair of moon-bright wings swept overhead. Webster gasped excitedly, and whispered, urging me to shoot.

I raised the gun deliberately, taking my time, puzzled by the unearthly apparition I saw at the outer limit of the flashlight beam. I squeezed the trigger, and the report of the weapon was followed instantly by a sound high above.

It was a human scream – a woman's cry – of pain and shock.

The wings pulsed, describing a tight, frantic circle. The tranquilizer was slow to bring her down – although I had used enough Phazadine to knock out a buffalo. A feather spun, and lanced the ground at our feet, an upright, silver-bright plume.

When her wings folded, their strength failing, unable to beat against the wind, she clung to the column of the broken eucalyptus with her claws, scrabbling and struggling. I believed, against my better judgment, that I was hearing human speech from above, cries of regret and dismay. I could not understand the words, but I had an uncanny sensation that I had heard such speech before.

She glanced downward, and I caught a glimpse of eyes glittering in the flashlight beam, a pain-stricken countenance. I also got the quick impression of beauty — human beauty. I was heartsick to have wounded her, even so slightly.

She tried to climb higher, her finger-like claws tearing the bark of the old tree. She slipped downward, and at last fell tumbling to the ground.

She took me in with gray eyes, her mouth working to speak. She spat sounds, but I was unable to gather any meaning from them, nor make any sense at all of what I was seeing.

I retreated — the single shot from my rifle having been spent I was rendered defenseless. The dart glittered from one tawny haunch, and she snatched at it, catching it in a claw, sending the dart spinning into the darkness.

"We only want to help you!" cried Webster, although his actions belied this statement. The heavy revolver was in his grasp, held in both hands, pointed steadily at our quarry.

"Matthew, why can't you find out what's wrong?" said our quarry, in clear, unmistakable English. I was thrilled and sickened. She knew my name! And what was even more telling, she spoke in an accurate imitation of my late wife.

[5]

IT WAS THE QUESTION Esther had asked me in the hospital, while her voice was still strong and clear, before the fatally deep sleep captured her.

Indeed, I found out what was wrong too late, when isolating the spores and discovering a medical defense against them could no longer help my stricken beloved.

"Webster, how did you manage to find a sphinx?" I found myself asking when the creature succumbed, in stages of drowsy decline, to the powerful tranquilizer. Webster hung the sturdy flashlight from a thicket, so the beam illuminated the clearing.

I approached her, unwilling to touch her, the way sometimes I had been afraid or reluctant to lay a hand on a lioness or a drug-stunned grizzly. There is something unfair about taking advantage of such animal power brought low, even when our human intentions are innocent, or even benevolent toward the creature's health.

She possessed the head of a woman, with flowing sea-dark locks, and the tawny body of a well-muscled feline, just a little smaller than an African lioness. Her nearly hand-like claws were tipped with gleaming ebony, and her wings, now that they were folded close to her body, were marble-pale. As I looked at her, however, I realized that her features were not quite human. Some unearthly, uncanny quality made her, in repose, look vaguely Homo sapien, but not like any person I had ever seen.

Or perhaps they did resemble one person – I could not be sure.

"I didn't find her," said Webster after a long silence. "They found me – and I thought I could trap this dangerous one, and keep her."

I made a weary gesture, urging him to tell me what he knew.

"The sphinxes accosted travelers," said Webster. "And unless they correctly responded to a riddle, they became the sphinx's lunch."

"There were more than one of them?"

"There were more than one," he said succinctly. "At least two."

"I didn't know they could fly," I said.

"I was surprised they could speak English," he said. "They are creatures dedicated to surprising the likes of us. The first one I encountered stopped me on a donkey path on Cos, up near the temple to Athena. Do you know what she asked me?"

"I couldn't guess."

"Well, never mind." He drew back the hammer on the revolver. "This one here — you know what we have to do."

I realized how close he was to taking her life, leaning forward, pressing the gun against her head.

"You can't shoot her," I protested.

"I have to."

"She's a sentient being," I said, pushing him away.

"No, Matthew," said Webster, trembling with emotion but looking very much like a man who would have his way. "This is not the wise sphinx. This one is a monster who only seems to speak."

I considered this. "It certainly sounded like human speech to me."

"No again," responded Webster. "She was imitating something in your memory. They are cunning creatures. Not to be trusted. And think about it — did it really sound like Esther?"

"It was close enough."

"It was a little singsong, wasn't it?"

"Maybe she has trouble speaking English."

"This is the beast that tore my leg last week," Webster said. "From hip to knee, all the way to the bone."

"That's dreadful, Webster," I said, "but think what a rare creature she is."

"Not nearly rare enough," said Webster with an ugly, unhappy laugh. "I believe she accosts people up and down the mainland, Matthew. And when they don't say the right thing she kills them. And then she consumes their flesh."

I could not deny the possibility, and the stars above us, and the rugged, moonlit landscape all around, seemed to radiate a great chill, as though a wind blew upward out of the earth. I could not bear the thought of destroying a beautiful marvel, but I knew I had to help preserve human lives.

The pistol's report, when it came, was far away. I did not associate it with the sigh that had erupted from Webster just before the pistol-crack reached my ears.

"Ah!" Webster exclaimed again, like a man responding to a mnemonic clue. "I think – " He patted himself, dropping the revolver.

"Matthew, I do believe," he added, a man at last recalling something clearly, an essential *aha* experience that, at the same time it focused his thoughts, wearied him greatly. "Matthew, I do believe I have been shot."

[6]

ANACLETTE STEPPED into the clearing just as I helped Webster sink to his knees, and lie down on the damp ground. The holster at her hip was empty – the automatic pistol was in an unmittened hand I could not bring myself to more than glance at.

"We can still save him," I said.

I was aware that it was unwise or even absurd to ask a woman who had, by all evidence, just shot her husband to join in any effort to preserve his life. Nevertheless, Webster Brentwood had been a marvel in his own way, unique and bristling with life, and I was appalled as he gurgled and gasped his last few moments.

He died in my arms.

"Poor Webster," said Anaclette, holstering her weapon. "He knew so much, and yet what did he really know?"

"This is outrageous, Anaclette," I heard myself say as I climbed to my feet. Like many people before me, I retained an unwarranted faith in words as I continued, "Why did you shoot him?"

But I had already seen enough. I knew that I was about to be killed. I had a quick preview of what I could do next.

I could seize the magnum-force-six gun from the ground, and put Anaclette under lock and key somewhere in the house.

But then my plan petered out.

I had no clear way to hold her prisoner. Not while the fabulous winged companion at the outer edge of the circle of light was already beginning to murmur in her drug-borne sleep, and stir.

"Help me put the shackles on her, dear Matthew," said Anaclette.

I watched as she gave up on receiving my help, and tugged the drowsing creature toward the iron post in the shadows. The manacles clicked, and then Anaclette rejoined me, putting an arm around my waist, like a seductive hostess at a party.

"You have nothing to fear, Matthew my love," she said. "Didn't you already answer my riddle?"

I have never been so afraid — or so unable to conceive a coherent thought — in my life.

"The riddle," I finally managed to respond, "about the tide."

"And you helped," she continued, "to save my dangerous, quite treacherous sister's life."

I must have asked a question, or perhaps she read the wonder in my eyes. She gave a gentle laugh, and as she leaned into me I sensed the stirring of a wing, hidden under her mantle. "Matthew, neither my sister nor I are mortal."

"What are we going to do with Webster?" I asked.

The unplanned use of the plural pronoun was not lost on either of us.

"You go on," she said, "up into the house, dear Matthew."

"We can't just leave him here."

"Didn't I tell you," she said with a smile, "that sometimes I get very hungry?"

Mrs. Big

after "Jack and the Beanstalk"

SOMETIMES I COMPLAINED too much, but there was a lot to complain about.

We couldn't live in the village among the blacksmiths and the potters. We shook the ground when we tiptoed, and every time we napped in the town square we rolled over and crushed the Charter Oak or the Stone of Justice, or some other ancient monument beloved by man and boy. Our burps shattered windows in the chapel, and my stifled sneezes slopped duck ponds dry.

I started telling him it was all the fault of the peewee Englishmen, so tiny their yells were squeaks. I flattened an ox by mistake one morn, out shaking dust off a doily. The ox-drovers cried out in terror, bovine mush all over my instep.

"The Englishmen are too small," I said. "And not only that, the Englishmen are thieves!" This was the truth, as all giants know. Our kind always have some few tons of gold dust or silver nuggets tucked away, and we were always brushing away a couple of carter's boys or tanner's apprentices, trying to steal nodes of ore the size of bishops.

One evening, out watching the full moon come up, I trod on a milkmaid, and I knew then we had to make changes. It was bad enough having to scrub girl-juice off my best wooden shoe.

It was the way my husband took it so hard that really troubled me. He brooded for days on why people-folk are so minuscule and easy to squish. And as tough as I like to sound, I don't like squashing maidens any more than you would.

Little by little his usual complacent, happy nature started to go sour. Before, he had been glad to wave at a passing hayward, off to guard the sheaves. Now he frowned, and stuck out his lip, and started the beginnings of his famous poem.

"I smell an Englishman," he would declare, a picnic of villagers scrambling out of his shadow. "I smell the blood of an Englishman," he would sing out, shaking his fist the size of a cow barn.

I encouraged him. "You smell the blood of a mite, is what you smell," I said. "A bunch we'd be well rid of." The wee folk had a strong scent, charred beef and tobacco, green ale and cheddar. You could nose a gentleman farmer and his lady half a league away.

I had hoped my beloved would be one of the Raving Giants, terrors of the earth, and devour the citizens of the countryside, like my great uncle, scourge of Europe. I'd hoped he'd be a Bard of the Big, like a few of my forebears. But instead he was a garden-giant, planting oaks and patting the earth around their roots. He had fine gold in bags of whale skin stitched together, and silver in schooner sails, but otherwise he was more peaceful planter than monster.

One day he hurried home with a gleeful expression, poplars shivering at his tread. He announced, in a voice that gave a flock of passing geese a collective heart attack, "I've found a home!"

He'd bought it from a traveling peddler for a pocketful of

pumpkins, he explained. It was acreage with a view, a manse, plenty of garden-space, but with one drawback from the point of view of access: it was in the clouds.

"What sort of peddler?" I thought to ask, but could not get the words out in my wonderment and concern.

We had to stack carriages, oxcarts, sheds, and steeples one on top of each other, a teetering column, just so we could clamber up and take possession of the place. Once there, the pile tumbled back to earth with a dusty crash, and we were homeowners.

"What sort of peddler indeed!" I had cause to think in days and weeks to come.

If I walked beyond where the wash was hanging, blue and yellow in the sun, I'd stumble and there it would be, the land way down there, cloud spinning-off right under my feet. We feasted on gourds, squash, marrow, courgettes, that race of veggies that grows big. When the cloud-land parted, some of the yams tumbled down, all the way to the countryside below. He would patch the cloud-field with some more of the stuff we walked around on, and rake it neat.

The view from the manse was all thunderhead and sun, and sometimes a bird would make it all the way up to where we lived. He would alight on one of the melon plants that grew like weeds and peep around at things, bright and chirpy. I was learning to be a wiser giantess, and learned not to complain so much, even when my husband made up more of his poem, the verses of which could get on a plaster Virgin's nerves.

"I smell the blood of an Englishman," he would say, and then try out the words, "Peas, cows, drakes, drums, I smell the...." Or other random verbal assortments, until I wanted to scream.

My father was the Giant Poet of the East, renowned among the deepest valleys for his alliterative verse. He's the wit who made up such famous phrases as shilly-shally, hale and hearty, vim and vigor, and other such word-pairs.

I explained the importance of form over meaning, of nonsense over simple declaration, and my husband, the poor dear, took it so to heart he sulked. This pained me, because the truth is I was growing very fond of my huge hubby, isolated in the sky though we were.

His earnest humming in the cuke patch, his merry "Blood of an Englishman" yodel, all worked him ever deeper into my heart. I came to regret that I'd ever been critical in the first place. So when he burst in on me as I darned his breeches, and blurted out, "I smell the blood of an Englishman! Fee, Fie, Foe, Fum!" I clapped with appreciation, and patted his pink cheek.

I should have kept my mouth shut. "But wouldn't it be better back to front?" I began. And when he beamed, uncomprehending, I continued, "With the 'Fee, Fie' part first in the poem, the 'blood' part second?"

Such a sulk I have never observed in man or giant, a sulk of such deep duration I was afraid he would never speak again.

Long days and somber nights he tugged the weeds, watered the crookneck and the summer squash with squeezed cloud, wrung-out like sponges on the leafy vines. He met my eyes with sorrow, bearing up, brave-hearted, but thinking he had failed me, knowing how my family prized a turn of phrase. So there we were, solemn and quiet, when the terrible thing happened.

One day I was wringing the suds from my husband's knickers, and the next a human flea was squeezing through a hole in the cloudy field. Not one of the usual wear-and-wind holes, either, but a puncture made by a bean vine with leaves as big as me. I couldn't scream, I couldn't take a breath.

The lad was quick, and like a weevil he crept along the garden path, but by then my husband straightened in the garden, sniffing. Sniffing the bright air he said, softly, "Fee, Fie, Foe, Fum. I smell the blood of an Englishman." Gentle, like it was a love poem, an offering from his heart.

Then he frowned. "I do!" he exclaimed. "I smell — "

He gathered himself, put one foot forward and sang out, for all under the sky to hear, "Fee! Fie!" And continued on to declaim his entire, famous poem, the one they heard from Iceland to Crete that very instant.

We couldn't find the boy. The human pup got lost in the hall, and lost in the pantry, and lost in the parlor, too. All over the manse we sniffed him out, but not a glimpse could we see.

Human as he was, I should have known. A giant's footstool, a god-sized spoon, a magnificent pair of breeches drying over a chair the size of a county were nothing to an English lad. He sought gold. He squirted through the chest-chamber, leaped up the side of a cask of gold, and bounded high, onto a sack the size of a guildhouse. He was a leaping-lad, digging and cutting with a cunning little knife, gold dust like summer wheat pouring out upon the floor.

He stuffed his breeches pockets with as much gold as he could cram, and leaped more slowly, jumped and scrambled. And then he stumbled, weighed down with 24-karat powder, and rolled under my feet. In my fear that I might flatten him dead on the spot, I lifted one foot. I shifted another. I swayed.

I swung my arms, and fell with a crash that shook the cloudland and shivered the billowing cumulus from north to south.

My husband caught my look of pain, his eyes filled with shock at my distress, and ran after the human speck, bellowing the poem.

The thief was clumsy, fat with gold, escaping the grasp of my angry spouse by a feather's span. I hurried after the two, gasping that I was not hurt, but now, when I wished my words had weight, they had no effect on large or small. The thief heaved himself to the stalk and shinnied down, leaf to leaf, falling, catching himself, until he was out of sight.

My husband hesitated – no giant can scramble, or bound, or spring to save his life. He took a deep breath, and clambered down, swaying the mighty beanstalk, leaves thrashing, covering the sound of my cry that I was all right, that my loved-one need not avenge me. The thief had scampered all the way down to the landscape before my husband had mastered his grip on the leaves, and the thief began to work with a tiny ax, far below.

Who has not heard the story? How my husband fell, crashing through the green into the flat and distant earth? How Jack – for even robbers have names – hugged his mum and bragged of gold, and three beans exchanged with a peddler for a cow. While my husband lay like a hill, a mountain shaped like a man, stretched out with his last glance bright with love for me.

Fear not, Jack and Jack's mother, I wanted to say. Stay calm, villagers and geese. I sought no vengeance on a foolish lad, or harm to roof or heath. And be not afraid of my story's end, or believe it tells the demise of my beloved.

Even then I spied the creature I wanted, stealing down the hedgerows, the single cause of all my grief. I hurried after him, my shadow flowing ahead of my stride.

Sorcery that can ennoble the clouds with an estate, and sprout a beanstalk to heaven from three beans, can cure a giant poet of a fall. I sought the scurrying peddler with his magic wares.

He ran across a cow pasture, fled across a barnyard, staggered through daisies.

And I followed easily, bending, reaching. He was far too slow.

Give Him the Eye

MARINERS COMPLAIN about the weather, the sea-current and the gods, and they have a low opinion of each other, as well. Sometimes these salt-stained men start fighting, right down along the shore here, engaging in two-fisted brawls, and sometimes they spill blood.

You'd think they'd be ashamed to disturb the peace, this charming, olive-tree-lined inlet being something in the way of a tourist attraction, after all, but you see boatmen taking a swing at each other, and then kicking and pelting each other with stones, and what are they fighting about?

Mooring stakes, almost always – the pegs high up on the pebbly beach. That is what all the trouble is about. Men get bloody knuckled over who gets to tie up to the biggest and best mooring stake, and my sisters and I can't believe the childishness. We've seen hundreds of years of this, so who are we to get excited, but the other day we finally had seen enough, just after the squall that blew the ship onto the Sinis Rocks, passengers and merchants all over the place, and coughing up water and drowning, too, you wouldn't believe the grief.

A portly, bearded fisherman – one Ponteus, of nearby Samos – had caught a bushel of whitebait, pretty little fish but nothing exciting. He had to hurry to haul the little fish to market because of the black and white gulls keening overhead. The fowl were getting hungry at the sight of all the still-living fish, wiggling and splashing, a great basket of finny creatures about to be eaten entirely by the hungry seabirds.

Ponteus means, translated roughly, *Seaman*, and this fisherman was justly proud of his name. He lived up to it, too. He hauled his keel as far up the beach as he could, and then ran up toward the stake, just in time to get himself into a footrace with a Piraean pilot, who just dropped by with his wife and children to see the famous sisters.

People from Piraeus, let's face it, can be troublesome. They think that because they are from the main port of Athens and they speak with that upper-crust Attic accent they can just about get what they want out of life.

This tall, good-looking Piraean, his silk tunic going swish-swish-swish as he hurries along, realized he was about to get beaten to the biggest mooring stake. He ran harder, so hard you could see the little veins in his forehead. He reached the stake first, and it is a nice tall stake, as tall as he is, and shaped like our Greek letter *tau,* not bent over and stumpy like some of the other boat-ties along the beach.

The pilot, his trade identifiable by the red-dyed cap he was wearing, turned and cheerfully called out to his wife and two little toddlers, "I got the stake, Xuthus, bring me the rope."

The little sparrow-like wife lives up to her name, Xuthus meaning "little brown nondescript winged fowl." She struggled with the tarry coils while the fisherman bustled up to the prized mooring stake.

Wasting not a moment, Ponteus backhanded the Attic seaman, tied one of those triple knots you would need a sword to cut through, and there was the Attican embarrassed in front of his family, his face smarting, staggering to his feet and feeling just about ready to fight back.

Which he did, and there were the two men punching and cursing, right in front of the little knurl where my sisters and I hold court during the tourist season. Some call it a cave, but I say it's a knurl, which I think is a nicer word, don't you?

It's just a little rocky overhang, and a sheltered place we have fixed up pretty handily with some woven kelp and some sheepskin seats and we've made it into a comfy spot, if I may say so. When travelers visit us they are always a little surprised and they say, trying to put it nicely, "Why, I expected a hovel and here you are, with a little shelter done up as-pretty-as-you-please."

It has little pebbles you can buy for a bead or a helmet-shell fragment, anything colorful — we aren't that fussy. You can take them home to your villa along the Aegean and say, "Yes, one of the Graiae — the Gray Ones — gave it to me."

We used to sell olives, but people were put off by the fact my sister Pemphredo kept dropping our eye into the olive jug, fishing it out with a cackle and chewing it up, only to surprise young and old alike by showing that she had just palmed the eyeball and wasn't really eating it.

You have heard about us, the three sisters born old and doomed to live forever, Pemp being the clown, Dino being the melancholy one, and me being the one with all the sense. We had one eye between us from the beginning, although we had everything else we needed. Our father Phorcys sired all the sea serpents in the ocean — if you run across a sea monster he's a half brother of mine.

Soon wearied of the sight of this sweaty brawl, I leaned on my stick and shuffled along down to where the two men were struggling.

"Leave be," I pronounce, in old-fashioned Greek, the way I have heard Athena speak it.

They fought unabated.

"Leave the peace unsullied, mortals," I add, poking the eye back in with one gnarled finger.

It rolls out — I can't get it to fit quite as well as Pemp can when she uses it, and Dino has given up trying except when Aphrodite stops by, quite a show when she arrives with her entourage, if I may call it that.

The pilot, at least, had the sense to stop fighting. He recognized me. We are, after all, a peculiar and distinctive trio, my sisters and I, with graceful forms, swan-like, but frail with inhuman age from the moment of our births.

"I beg your pardon, undying one," said the pilot, out of breath but remembering his manners.

The fisherman turned to me and said, "Get away, you old hag."

My two sisters back under the knurl gasp at the sound of this, and Dino says, incredulously, "What did he say?"

Pemp is livid. "Old *what?*" she is sputtering.

Some say we have only one tooth between us, and I like that story, just to show I have a sense of humor. One tooth! That would be funny, wouldn't it, eating sesame cakes with one yellow bicuspid.

We three are challenged when it comes to teeth, but each of

us has our own, thank you for your interest. I showed all of mine that instant in a not very friendly smile and cupped a hand to my ear, as though I had not heard him quite clearly.

"You miserable, bent-back crones, shut your mouths," says the fisherman.

"What?" pipes Dino. "What did the fisherman say?"

Pemp, who likes to roll herself into a ball and somersault, crippled as she is, by way of entertaining children, was furious — not because the fisherman thought we were contemptible, but because he thought we were mortal.

If you are going to curse a mortal, do it for just cause, is the policy I prefer to follow. I hunched closer yet.

"What did you say, my good fellow?" I asked, using my other voice — my lovely sound.

This unexpected tone of voice stopped Ponteus the fisherman for a moment.

It is the sound of a temptress. Aphrodite herself taught me a song once, sang it with me, and she then told me my tones were purest argentum. The goddess has no reason to exaggerate.

Ponteus was shaken.

He looked me up and down. He reckoned the likelihood of my being able to do anything to hurt him, nonetheless, and the sunburned, bearded seaman liked his odds.

He said something of such unvarnished coarseness that the pilot turned away in disgust with his fellow mortal. The Piraean led his small family away as the fisherman, sure that he had gone too far, and yet intoxicated by his own bluster, gave me a kick. It was not a hard blow — just a breath of sand on my worn and weathered shin.

Words are alive.

Alive, and rich with power. Given a lovely name, a child may be quickened by its character into courage, or a compassionate nature. Given a harsh name, a boy might strive to make it into something more than dross, so that he may become noble in nature by disproving an awkward *nomen.*

My name is Enyo — Warlike.

"Ponteus," I said. "Let us change your name. Let us know you forevermore as Dysponteus."

Pemp laughed, always one to love a joke.

Ponteus gaped, unsure what to make of such a new, unpleasant name.

WHEN PERSEUS the hero arrived that morning on his way to slay the Gorgon he thought of himself as bold and cunning.

But his name means "destroying one," and he was living out the power and, at the same time, the dark fate with which his name endowed him. The Gorgon was our sister, and yet we told her slayer where she lived. He went forth from us to cut off her head, that famous hero, his destiny aided by the immortal gods.

Did he steal your eye, some will ask? Is that true?

One of my sisters wept as I pointed out the path for him, and the other mocked the young man's seacoast accent, but I knew that one day his bones would be washed by the cold salt sea. He was mortal, and the round and passing years would prove more powerful than youth.

THE MOON was peaceful and the sun merry.

Days slipped by after the fight between the fisherman and the pilot, and one afternoon the village elders organized a gift basket for us, with fig-wine and honey cakes. Unlike some of the tourists who arrive here, fat and loud, the folk whose great-grandparents saw us as we are now approach us with trepidation, and they are afraid to offend us.

Especially me.

"We thank you for your help, honorable Gray Ones, in saving so many of the survivors of the recent shipwreck," said one of the elders, withered and white-bearded, and yet a thousand years younger than we three.

"We rescued them because they made such noise," said Pemp with mock-sourness, "with all their screaming out in the water."

"It grieved us," said Dino, "to hear the little ones crying."

I accepted the gift of cakes and wine.

"We asked our brothers of the sea to help," I said simply. "My sorrow is that we could not save each mariner and merchant, or keep each child from being orphaned."

It's true – Perseus took our eye, and threw it into the water, eager to destroy more than he needed to win his quest.

But the nearby villagers found the bloodshot orb, and brought it back to us safe and whole. They are thoughtful neighbors, if wary.

Some will find our lingering on, century upon century, grotesque or sad. Or find our tale amusing, in a horrid way, as though the ownership of a single, far-seeing eye is not enough for three who have seen more than they need of human woe.

I heard a cry this morning, a grief struck wife, and a wailing child – sounds which sorrowed Dino and gave me no joy, either.

My fisherman had washed up at dawn, conquered by the name I had given him. The man once named proudly after the sea I renamed after the stormy waters that rose to swallow him.

Thanks to me, *Ponteus* became *Dysponteus*, and as a result the bearded mariner tangled in his own net and drowned in a rainy squall.

Like so many, my fisherman believed that what we do is more important than what we say.

The poor man, foolish despite his vigor. Perhaps he never realized that, when breath is still and the last eye stolen, it is our words that sing.

Medusa

SHARP-EYED ATHENA passed among us in those days.

From shore to hilltop, little was lost on her. She was quick to spot someone attempting an unwise deed, a youth walking along the rim of a well — showing off to a maiden — or a young woman flirting with a grinning brigand just arrived on a wine ship from Samos.

The goddess of wisdom, Athena was the winged shadow who brushed the ankle just enough to tumble the lad into the well, where his cries echoed until cold water drowned them. She was the owl-shape keening lustful encouragement to the shepherd's daughter, leaving her, as time passed, pregnant and bitterly wise.

Athena was a pretty little night-bird when she took to the wing, just avoiding the snapping jaws of the vixen or the hound, too sure of herself to be afraid of a hunter's tooth. In her womanly guise, the goddess was beautiful, with a laugh like warm wind in olive trees, her step gentle music among the small, white stones.

Every mortal woman learned to leap quickly from her path as the Daughter of Zeus came flirting with some demigod or human, running her hands through her sky-bright hair, her laughter causing red poppies to flower in the field.

I was a shipwright's daughter, my hair gilded by the sun. I spent my girlhood holding a plumb line and handing my father a wood-plane, helping my brothers peg planks to a ship's frame, loving my father and my brothers as the keel loves sea.

I learned the names of the winds as I grew up, my stature increasing with the summers. My shadow on the sand transformed from a girl's shape to a woman's. The wind ran through my tresses, breeze stroking my linen mantle so the outline of my still-maturing body was clear. I ran along the edge of the surf, chasing my brothers, laughing with them in the tart salt spray.

Handsome plowmen greeted me, cowherds offered me foaming cups of milk, and the wealthy vineyard keeper sang for me.

I was loved.

ONE DAY as I washed the sandy grit from my white feet, the tide began to rise. Sea rounded my ankles, lapping upward to my knees, the simmering brine chuckling, "Medusa, pretty Medusa, most lovely and playful of all the mortal maidens, listen to me."

My breath caught, and I stepped back. But I could not escape far, followed by the bubbling laughter of the foam, sporting with me, each step. It tickled pleasingly, this splashing froth. Who was I to flee?

And how could I deny the salt-silvered figure of Neptune in my bedchamber that night?

Strong-muscled, ancient, and ever-youthful Neptune, the sea god himself murmured into my ear his vows of faithfulness. He said that he believed himself in love, and I think he was. My room grew bright with sea-joy.

I heard her wings when they were still far off.

I recognized the flutter of her search, circling as she spied his wet steps among the grasses of the dunes, her feathers cutting through the night.

My chamber curtain wafted and parted, flung aside by a pair of owl wings.

I knew her at once, the silken plumage, those gray, raptor eyes, seeing what was happening just as Neptune took me in his arms, the ocean god breathing my name like the surf.

An owl's cry split the hush, her shriek a curse.

My hair intertwined, locks seeking each other, coursing curls thickening, writhing. I could not make a sound, stunned. Arrayed across my pillow, my hair was a crown of serpents, each reptile hungry, rooted in my skull.

In his horror, Neptune fled me, his sea-perfume fading through the dark. Athena's voice, cold as any betrayed mortal woman's, whispered, "From this night, Medusa, every man who sees you will turn to stone."

Every lover, I thought she meant, never dreaming the weight of a goddess's curse.

At dawn, terrified of my own twisting shadow, serpents lunging, battling one other, I cried out for my father. He called my name in return, interrupted as he fastened on his shipwright's apron.

He gaped in dismay.

And froze, just as he was, early morning glittering on the marble arms of his fatherly embrace.

I called out, "Not one step closer, I pray you," to my brothers.

They rushed forward, aroused by my shriek, and they, too, cast suddenly unmoving shadows, their once-quick features forever in white stone.

I hid among the sand dunes and the brambles, my serpent diadem darting, anchored in my head, ever-hungry, lashing the air before my eyes. I went without food. I slept among the roots of trees, and drank from black-scummed brooks. When my sandals wore thin, I cast them off and tattered my soles on thorns. I cried out to warn wandering shepherds, and hissed to frighten hunters. Spring and fall, I felt no human touch.

The story is told as far as the round sea's end, how Athena, even that sky-dwelling divine, sickened at the sight of her curse's handiwork. Regret or disgust ripened in her, until one day she found a champion.

She stroked his arm, and seduced him into courage. Bold Perseus, he of the sharp sword and ready laugh, was sailing forth to cut off my head.

I heard the village-folk murmur these tidings at the wellhead, ox-drivers repeating the rumor. I hid among the ancient olive trees and stole along the village paths, as far as I could wander from the frieze of stone men, my family and the occasional traveler, rooted to the soil, permanent and lost.

I devised a plan.

The lonely have months to study the nature of the gods, and the nature of false wisdom. I heard Perseus singing, coming for miles, love songs about Athena. He had a voice that charmed. He strode through the groves carrying his mirrored shield, adorned by divinely inspired confidence, and circled around by a pair of darting, moon-silver owl wings.

I had heard it foretold by shepherd's gossip, how he had polished his shield so he could eye my reflection without harm, how Athena would guide his sword-arm, murmuring in his ear, in love with the songs about her own eternal beauty.

He smiled when he saw me in his shield.

He spoke my name — he was so in love with his own voice.

"I wish you good morning," he added, mock-formal, groping for the pommel of his sword.

I said nothing, saving my speech for the prayer I had crafted during my long silence.

A sure-footed man, one who had never questioned his own destiny, he winked as he kept my reflection in his shield. He slipped his sword from its sheath. The blade's shadow lifted, and he held it high as the owl breathed encouragement.

The sword whispered as it cut through the air.

WHEN PEOPLE SPEAK of me they tell of my head cut-off. They study statues and paintings of my demise, severed head held aloft, staring with wide eyes as my power to transform men ebbs away.

No one knows the secret.

How a darting pair of wings swooped, whispering praise to the swordsman as he swung the blade. The bright owl banked, gliding ever closer, the wind from her feathers arousing my serpent-crown.

A snake goes hungry like no other living creature. Starving, voiceless and unnamed, cool nights chill the reptile, and hot sun scalds her. Within the shadow of a living quarry at last, at least one pair of reptile eyes grew bright.

A famished snake snatched the owl. The hungry serpent swallowed, working the night-bird down, enclosing the struggling wings in her belly.

THE SHORE IS WHITE, and rippled with wind-dunes.

Sea strokes the sharp stones round. Centuries come, and the sharpest flint is softened, caressed by the tongues of surf.

Let me live, was my dying prayer to Athena, trapped in the muscled darkness of a snake.

Let me live as I deserve, I prayed, the sword stroke severing vessels and bone, my fading sight held high.

And I will let you go.

The goddess struggled, her sharp talons, her crushed wings, working – helplessly. And at that moment she was truly wise.

The wind from the north blows cold, and summer rolls blue and empty of song. Perseus is nothing, a graven hero, a breath of air.

Athena, in her desperation, made a vow.

And she keeps her word.

Now I am stone, among the rounded, enduring company of my father and my brothers. Every time you walk along the gray and dappled pebbles of the shore you hear us, laughing with the never-dying sea.

P-Bird

[1]

IT'S HOT HERE.

Men in suits drive down from Sacramento, and, with their black briefcases and gold ball-point pens, they get out of their air-conditioned state-government four-doors and you can see them hunch over, blinking from the sunlight.

They are polite, and soft-spoken, but they sound hard as they suggest, "You don't want to talk about what happened, do you Mr. Hanford?"

They say, "The government needs to keep some matters off to one side, out of the public view."

"You mean about top-secret zoological wonders? That sort of secret," I respond, "the sort the public should and will know about?"

They smile uneasily. They sigh.

They have their jobs to do. But you can see how disturbed they are. How frightened they feel, and how awestruck. You can see how merely mortal they realize they really are.

And how shocked they are at what happened.

[2]

SOME PEOPLE look at a turkey rancher and they think that whatever else bewildering might befall them in their lives they can say with joy lightening their footsteps: at least I am not a turkey man.

And my attitude is: let them think what they want. I walked tall, and bowed to no one. I was King of the Big Birds, Emperor of Turkeys, honcho of the witless fowl, and so good at what I did no one even bothered to envy me. My success was seen as natural, pure and straightforward. I was Turkey Tsar, and proud of it.

I was and in some ways remain a normal human being. Not for me the senseless swagger, or the snobbish acquiring of upmarket musical collections. I was just like you, but smarter and luckier – and then not.

I even have the best variety of education someone in my field could earn. I hold an MA in agricultural economics from the University of California, Davis, and while I affect a certain countrified drawl, and wear cowboy boots to the Lions Club pancake breakfast just like everyone else in the greater Fresno area, I can sit down and cozy up to the local English majors if I want to, and the pretty history teacher down the road became one of my special friends, if I may speak circumspectly.

I studied soil aridity and climactic alteration in class, but I funded my college years by working as a chef. I worked as a line chef at the Blue Bull in downtown Davis, searing tri-tips to a golden perfection, slicing and spicing potatoes. Eventually, I started my own catering service, Sam's Turkey and Other De-lites. After graduate school I became owner of a stylish eatery, T-Bird – short for Thunderbird, which is what the turkey had become to me, a source of life as well as prosperity.

I did fairly well.

It would not be bragging to go even further – I did very well.

I made a good deal of money, and because I was too busy to spend it, in a few years I was the toast of the Davis Chamber of Commerce.

Ever-increasing prices fattened my tax burden, while I honed my ability to chop and freeze and serve up a mean giblet mista con secret gravy and polenta with fungi and breast and whatever other specialties I could concoct from the domestic turkey.

The rep from the National Turkey Board (the guy who spearheaded the "Got Gobbler?" ad campaign, copied afterward by dairy folk and destined to become a catchphrase) used to drop by and marvel at my menu. He called me the Turkey Kingpin, joking but serious, too. He said, "Maybe some day you'll own a herd of turkeys yourself, Samuel."

I would chuckle, and call out, "Not for me the actual turkey, Hal."

Oh yes, I used to laugh in those days, while I fricasseed and braised and roasted the big, tasty, and inexpensive fowl. I had never seen one in the actual, wattled, and feathery flesh. Smart diners sought out my restaurant, inflating the prices on the menu, endive stuffed with elderberry and turkey confit going for thirty dollars as a starting dish. But I knew nothing of the grand poultry themselves, and was never tempted, even when Hal the turkey rep confided, "That's where the real brass is to be made, Sam – out there in among the turkey herds."

Yes, I laughed like any happy individual. But standing there in the sweaty kitchen, carving and roasting and stuffing and basting, I began to develop a dream of my personal destiny. Or perhaps it would be more accurate to say that the dream developed a hold on me.

I saw myself, in this vision, under the sky. It was big, bold, blue sky, and the horizon was far away. I stood astride the sun-warmed land and took a deep breath and said to myself something manly and steeped in a love of freedom.

Spreading out under the azure canopy was a herd — a flock, actually.

I can see the knowing smile creeping over the features of my open-minded but still fairly typical reader. What, Samuel, you will be thinking: no Texas longhorn. No black Angus, or half-wild mavericks. Your vision of the west is a herd of lowing, long-necked birds?

Well, I see that my slice of the American dream is a source of amusement, and I don't even trouble myself over it. Go ahead and laugh, I say, whoever chooses to do so. Chuckle and shake your head. I wanted a flock of the great gallinaceous fowl spread out before me, under my protection, and to the betterment of my personal prosperity and the nourishment of my country.

I sold my restaurant to a containerized-shipping mogul, searched the Central Valley, and found what I was looking for.

I said, "I'll fatten those big white birds and freeze them, and I'll be one happy man."

That is how I came to buy the Straits of Magellan Turkey Ranch fifteen miles north of Fresno, California. It came complete with flash freezing facilities and a packaging plant. I was going to master every aspect of the turkey, from inception to inspection and up to and including distribution. I was even buying a fleet of refrigerator big-rigs to trundle my product to the Safeway hub in Bakersfield.

I was all set.

It was no easy matter, and there was a little danger involved in certain aspects of the ranch. The flash freezing factory was a stern affair, all nitrogen tanks and white tubing. Liquid gas could freeze a jackrabbit solid in about one-tenth the time it took to say *freeze*. That earnest and likeable inspector, Geoff Middles, you heard of during one especially brutal heat wave one year – he got caught in my ice plant.

It was a cruel day, the way it gets in the long summers of the great Central Valley, and a long stretch of dutiful hefting of his clipboard had Geoff feeling weary. He opened the wrong door, ignored the OSHA-mandated warning signs, sat down on a quiet conveyor belt – and when his assistants found him he was a frozen health inspector, solid to the spine.

The packaging plant was quite a different sort of domain. People in a turkey packaging plant don't simply package the large birds. They parboil the plumage to the naked skin, sear the pinfeathers, gut the birds, wrap the giblets, chop and parcel the white m. from the dark m. They collect the heads and feet and culinarily uninteresting offal and right there, on the spot, manufacture it into turkey feed.

That feed is fresh and moist and ready to perk up even the life-weary old tom you use for his sturdy sperm and photogenic profile and not much else. Feed him some of the Straits of Magellan Turkey Ambrosia and the elderly creature will step right on up to the highest point of the turkey yard and let forth one of those half-musical gargles that so rightly make the *Meleagris gallopavo* famous.

I supply all this not entirely flattering caulking around my tale to let you know that I am as smart as the next guy, and that no one should feel superior to me on the account of savvy, nor feel that they themselves are naturally exempt from the sort of sky-wide disaster that stripped me of my prospects. I was clever and lucky, and disaster swept my schemes aside.

I was the former kitchen wizard from a college town, newly arrived to a turkey ranch in the middle of California's nowhere. I had a yearly flock of thousands of prime, hybrid, transparent-hormone-enhanced bustards, and I was happy. I wore a three hundred dollar Stetson and custom boots and drove a retooled red Cadillac convertible with a roll bar and cordovan leather seats, the whole package of which I set flying over one hundred and twenty down Interstate Five one New Year's Eve. I was on the cover of *Poultry Economist* and for three years running I wrote a well-received column for *Scientific American Agriculturist*.

I married the bright-eyed history teacher on the other side of the Interstate from here, and Annie Jean and I were one smiling couple, season after season. I grew. I prospered. And then.

And then the storm came.

[3]

THERE ARE TWO MATTERS of common understanding regarding my tale which are completely true and which will come as no surprise to anyone.

One is that the weather of California's vast, flat interior is sometimes treacherous. We get the notorious ground fogs of winter — the so-called tule fog. The fog starts on nearly the same date every year — December 28. It lasts until dozens of passenger cars have been crumpled in chain reaction wrecks on the freeway, and people have despaired of ever seeing the sun or even the front yard ever again by the time February expires.

We get the staggering summer heat, and we get the winter downpours. And we get tornadoes.

Funnel clouds, twisters, gully-ticklers, path-blasters. We don't boast of legions of the twisting winds the way Iowa does, but we have our own special breed of the evil winds and they do real damage.

The other aspect of my story that is a matter of common understanding is: the turkey is an unintelligent bird.

This is true. The hen and the tom alike are as witless as can be. I have seen turkeys march in single file into a water tank and drown until water overflowed and the tank was solid with dead birds.

I have seen turkeys blown into a heap by a wind, and suffocate, tangled and squabbling, until they were all lifeless by the several hundreds. A passing biplane cropduster – an aircraft that the gobblers have seen every day of their lives – will, for no knowable reason, start the birds into a panic. They will all, every single one of them, stampede into a corner of the feeding pen and give up the ghost. The ones on the bottom of the pile will surrender to mortality first, and the ones on the top last, out of solidarity, it would seem, with their recently deceased cousins. But die they all will, as though quite on purpose, and to the rue of the turkey rancher.

To me this feckless lack of cerebration made *el pavo* seem all the more precious to me. The bird needs my help, I thought. I felt sorry for the creature. It cannot live, I thought, without my feeding and watering and daily and nightly protection. I loved my birds.

The weather that particular spring was a challenge. We saw rain, and we had puddles like lakes. We saw frost and we slipped on acres of ice. We knew harsh wind, and we endured hail.

And then came the tornado.

My flock was already depleted. Many had died looking up at the precipitation, drinking it in until they drowned. Some died of fright when the hail came down. Others died out of sympathy. I still had some healthy birds left, but the twister finished them all off, down to the last, grumpiest tom.

"Sam, come quick!" called Annie Jean.

I was in the office, toggling my spreadsheets. I had not taken out nearly enough storm insurance, and was facing something like a bleak prospect that morning. I left my computer and I ran all the way out to the livestock pen and looked upward.

The twister dangled down from a slate-blue cloud, drifted lower, and began making a noise like a giant wind coming down out of the sky with the intention of killing what was left of Samuel Hanford's turkeys.

The funnel cloud drew nigh, just as Annie Jean and I fled to the shelter of the tractor shed. The black, howling force of nature scoured the turkey yard of every last bird, and took them all, every one of them. The wind acted as though it possessed a sense of purpose. It sorted back around the water tank for a last cowering hen, before the storm swanned off toward the south taking all my birds, and all my livelihood. I was, within a few dreadful moments, destitute and bereft.

A storm followed, a tempest of such violence that the employees in the packing plant let out howls of fear and sorrow, expecting to lose their lives. The day drew murky, lightning lashed the sky. It was the latest and last, shocking word in bad weather.

When it had passed, and the calm of a placid afternoon descended, we crept out from our improvised shelters, and beheld a giant.

It was a huge red-winged wonder, dead and spread out, all over my stricken ranch. The storm had stricken and dumped a wondrous beast, a bird so big that even at a brisk walk, starting at its beak, it took me ten minutes to reach its wingtip.

I was a sudden pauper, in economic danger, and I had to use my mental powers. I was experienced at dinner hour improvisation, having survived a few hectic evenings as a chef. I considered for a long moment, and then I turned to Annie Jean and said, "Don't worry – we'll be fine."

She gave me a hopeful look, laced with skepticism.

"We'll rise up, as it were, from the ashes," I said.

I spoke with an optimism I did not entirely possess.

But as soon as I said the words, the plan was firm in my mind. I ordered the gigantic bird cleaned, plucked, packaged, and frozen, and right away before anyone noticed this great bird had escaped from whatever refuge had once protected it/her/him.

The carcass was huge, and it took a good deal of effort. We labored into the night, and I will confess that I doubted at times that we could freeze and load all of the bird into the Straits of Magellan fleet of big-rig refrigerated trucks. But by the next morning we had done just that.

There is an aspect of my story no reader will anticipate, except for the wise among us, or the ones who have heard the rumors. As I stood beside my wife, my loving arm around her, and watched my fleet of trucks trundle down the two-lane, carrying away the tons of just-frozen (giant) poultry, the long line of trucks suffered a disturbing alteration.

They shimmered. They shivered, and the various drivers braked and turned, haphazardly, onto the shoulder of the road.

The trucks broke open, and with a breathy fluttery rumble, the thousands of fragments of packaged poultry rose up into the air.

The multitude of ascending bits of flesh assembled into a rough outline of a giant bird, and then into a congregation forming the definite, solid shape of such a creature, and then the red-winged phoenix rose even higher. Singing more beautifully than any music I have ever encountered, she flew westward.

And never returned.

[4]

THE MEN AND WOMEN from the government explain how much better it will be if I am quiet.

I see their point, and yet — what am I to do with a mountain of plumage, scarlet and auburn, gold and midnight blue, the left-behind plumes of the phoenix.

Already bits of it begin to blow from farm to farm, and I cannot help it if children gather the white, downy bits that spin along the ditches.

"Perhaps," says Annie Jean with helpful, hopeful air, "you'll think of something."

I smile. At night I can hear the music still, somewhere beyond the extinguished sun. I am not worried, although at an earlier point in my life by now I might well have despaired.

I'll sell the beautiful feathers, and thrive.

Or Be to Not

[1]

AT LAST.

And here I was beginning to think you would never notice me, you with your post-caffeine melancholy, your pre-cocktail ennui, your what's-next calumny against taking life as it comes.

It's come.

What a surprise for you, and now I confront your unbelief, your post-Christian horror of the Unseen World. You probably wonder how I can even catch your ear, after all this time, or worse – you don't believe in me at all.

It is I, Ophelia the Dane.

You thought I was drowned, after good-my-lord-Hamlet skewered my father like a rat and took off to the pirate-littered seas leaving me to addled senses and a heart bereft, my brother off studying Lucretius, the royal court flung front-to-back with undiscovered felony. So what's she doing, you're wondering, ready as you are for another nice long night of nice long night, what you call in your canon "living."

Alone, and aren't you feeling the pinch of it, this solitude?

Of course you are. And that paramour of yours is closeted, don't you think, with that chairman of the banquet, Professor

Boneblood. The man wined and feasted, whose wreath you ought to be wearing, Dean of All He Surveys.

You can't even hear me especially clearly, but even that little flaw in the chatter, that wrinkle in the white noise, that shadow over the over-lit floor space of your seven-days-a-week is enough to wrinkle the brow and have you beseeching the servant that attends you, "No, not another whinging relic, please."

As though your life is a constant courteous declining of another telemarketer from those under the strict arrest of Sergeant D. Be an honest auditor, for an instant. This has never happened to you before. No one has ever accosted you squeaking and gibbering in the California streets unless it happened to be simply another living soul.

This is something new in your experience, this startling wonder you already turn away from, pretending to be – what? Bored? Courageous? But let's imagine I catch you daydreaming, or pensive, or in such a disposition as to be identical to someone from England where they are all you-know-what.

You hear me right well enough, let us imagine, and know that you know what I am saying. "What's this voice I discern?" you ask the evening air, "this young woman who decided that *selvmord*" – as they call self-killing in the elegant and redoubtable rotten-kingdom tongue – "was plan A in her own personal future."

And if I could hear her at all, you wonder, why should I attend to this self-slaughtered little minx, and leave off my usual activity of seeming to live. Nay, auditor – you, sitting there putting on an I-am-not-listening disposition. You think you are living.

Let me bestir you to the truth.

You are deceived. You with your no-longer-so-youthful but

still pleasing countenance, your collection of books and artworks, music-providing machinery, and your air of having been cheated by life. You have been cozened, my lord. You should be chief of your department, captain of your company, and instead you are one of life's lieutenants, a left-behind.

You possess a likeable way of peering, of wondering as you reflect, pensive and reconsidering. You often assert, "I wish I were elsewhere." Is this why you withdrew the volume – little read these days by you, my lord – of verse plays and studied the old scenes, not reading so much as grazing along the ten-point printed page.

My lord, you are a gentleman, in short, and promise, against your will, to be a friend to a wandering spirit.

You are lonely and wronged and so, my lord, am I.

Nevertheless, I have more pulse in my watery presence than all of you, as a nation of living. And as to your peculiar claim to be alive: I am dead and the wind has grown weary that has erased my headstone but even so have more passion and wits and readiness than you, poor riddled-with-the-slings and whatnots.

Put down that vial of soporific medicine, accidental poison in a hasty hand, deadly in a cunning grasp. Don't insist to me that you have never dreamed of murder, and don't try to deaden the sound of me with drugs. And set aside your brandy-wine, the dearest vintage – there will be time for spirits and heart's ease yet to come.

Ask your servant to sound the alarm. See what a jest you play on yourself, my lord interlocutor against your desire. You have no servant. Or, to be plain, you are your own servant, lord of nothing. Look at the horologe bestride your pulse. Glance at it again. It is a habit of yours. Five minutes – not even five I have been here, as though by timing my visitation you will be able to counsel your physician or priest how many hours the Mistress of Hell drifted across your study.

You will say, "I have not time for this, daughter of the worthy Polonius, beloved of Prince Hamlet, young noblewoman. Alas, poor wraith," you would offer, "I am busy."

Busy! *The spurns that patient merit* you thought applied solely to you, impatient and barely meritorious. Look at you, already ready to climb from the pillow of comfort and exit. I am a ghost. I travel, and no cock's crow will stir me into stalking so the dawn does not quicken my –

[2]

ONCE MORE.

I visit again, stepping into this pleasing study with its books and engines of entertainment, the musical equipment and television silent. I attend a gentleman – I felt forlorn without his companionship.

My improvised shriver, my sole audience, my unwilling fellow pilgrim friend and fortune's slave, forgive me.

"There," I hear you say, "you see her, can't you?"

Can she?

Last night I either bored or offended you, and you bolted from the room. Tonight you have arranged a companion, holding your hand, squeezing it, causing those metacarpals a twinge. Your colleague in country matters, and yet where was she last night, my lord?

She was with quite another, and in no great degree of chastity, I can assert. More than simply unfaithful, she is any man's breakfast, the common suitor's lunch, the butler's supper.

Not quite your peer, is she, my lord? Blowsy silk, tight-binding trousers, and paint upon her face, her cheeks seconded by a blush no shame could cause to flower, and lips incarnadined by all that the deceiver's art can accomplish. To be blunt, my lord: you can do better than this.

But I have ascended from the shadows to ask your forgiveness. My lord and lady, I offer my apologies. I will be far more companionable this evening, and there is no need to gape at me.

You are not bounded by any force of man or nature. You are stout-hearted master of your days – forget whatever I uttered during our first audience. Would singing please you? Either of you? Both?

I can sing.

The centuries have not flattered my range or tone, but I could even this night steer the narrow passage of a tune. If it would please you. Although, the babbling lyrics penned for me in the play you will have seen or read or heard of – well, those sad songs were cheap stuff, really. Not equal to my spirit. Of course, I look back at that little reed of a girl, and I like to see her more the *klog kvinde* – the wise woman, as my country-folk would say – and not the broken-hearted trifle, out of her depth at last in the slow waters of prosody.

Shall I sing?

At least you are sitting quite still, the two of you. This is a pleasing sight, my lord and his easy lady. His lordship rose suddenly last night, and fled the room, anxiety in his features, and I felt that, even though it was in my power to hound my host, I should leave off. I restrained my humors.

My lord, I left you to a restless but I hope refreshing sleep, and all day I have not set foot within a room you inhabited. You had the freedom of your hours, and I know that you are grateful.

No need, indeed, no need to thank me, though the high speech is on your lips. My lord, I will not sing, but I will tell you the true story of a murder. I will disclose a mystery. I will tell of a monarch betrayed. You will be well pleased, will you not? I will do more, I shall act out upon you what it was like to lie still in the garden and have the poison poured into your entryway of hearing.

Let me act the murder out, in play, in illustrative jest, upon this new arrival, your lady.

And more, I will have you hear how I envision this, what the errant beads of this essence resembled, pearling upon the monarch's lobe. How can it be, you will ask, that this slip-of-a-gosling, this maiden, knows so much? The living thrive on tidings of murder, if the news travels far enough from one's own threshold. But can the dead, too, hunger for the details of such manslaughter?

I will be brief: I killed him.

I murdered the old king, the never-see-his-like again, my Hamlet's father. I was the one, teased into conspiracy by Claudius his brother, caught by his false wooing, little guessing it was Gertrude – buxom, bovine Gertrude – who would sit beside the usurper.

I am a murderess, come to tell all. This, surely, will win the favor of your willing audience. Lie down, my dear lady-wench, and I shall reenact that stealthy garden hour, birds and their feathery kin afoot and aloft. I shall –

But again you start up, both of you now, ashen and pushing me away, as though you could wave off the smoke from an adjoining table at a coffee shop, distraction in your aspect. Both of you tremble. I cannot feel your hands, waving me away, and follow you, my lord and lady polite but dispirited – I will not deceive you – wounded by your rude and sudden –

[3]

THREE OF YOU.

This third evening of my interview with you I encounter a restless, inquisitive, perhaps apprehensive trio.

My pale, besieged original host is present, with his unworthy lady friend, and who is this third counselor, a physician, is he, or a philosopher of the natural world, with his – what is that? A camera in his grasp, seeking to record my song? No music tonight, either, my friends, my trio of companions, but I have come prepared to answer any query you might make. He is drinking deeply of your rare spirits-of-wine and now I guess who he must be.

I know this man, this third presence in the room, this lover of too-expensive brandy.

This was not your idea, my gentleman, elsewhere-seeking friend. This idea was hers.

Hers was the plan for this evening's sport. "Oh, do let's ask Bonebody" – what is his name, in truth? – "head of the department, to see what a mad wreck you have become, my former darling."

Surely those aren't the words she chose, but she might just as well have said so. They are lovers, your hoyden and this chamber lizard, this lust maven, prince of the vain and empty.

But I will be well mannered. I will not startle. I will offer bounty.

In truth I have prepared a list of possible inquiries you might voice, any or all of which I shall respond – do put that away, Bonefish, that device. You'll find the circuits fused, the memory agog, if you do not encase your visual recorder this instant.

You can't hear me!

Or you can hear me, Bonefoot, but so faintly I am as the creaking of the roof beams overhead. This is why the plumes of smoke coil upward from the camera – new, was it, and just received from the hands of a helpful merchant?

Listen.

You begin to hear me now, taking in my words with a stirring of your breath, all three of you, sitting upright, frozen as it were. Unable to escape now, are you? Do I have your ears, my lords, my lady?

Queries I have arrived this evening prepared to entertain, including but not limited to the following:

a) How do I spend my days — nay, entire centuries — as a wandering wraith?

b) Does such a tireless, peace-stripped limbo await you, my still-quick fellow pilgrims?

c) Is it true, as I have asserted, that I murdered the good king?

d) Who authored the plays attributed to the playwright from Warwickshire, one William Shakespeare? Was it that famous but inexplicably enlightened inkster, or some other?

e) Why have I chosen you, of all others, to receive my attentions?

WHY ME, *why me*, isn't that the first question on any mortal's list?

Write the questions down, or any similar query you choose. I smile upon your curiosity and provide you with a page, an airy nothing to you but as solid as any slate to me. Write your questions down. You with the smoldering recording machine, write. My lady, write down what you seek to know. If you have the skill.

"For a moment or two," Bonecutter is saying, "I was beginning to wonder. But now I don't think there's anyone here but us," he adds, both deaf and cocky. "There is no one here but the three of us," concludes this departmental breed boar with a laugh, and she agrees, the vixen.

"Don't you think you should see a doctor, darling?" she whispers into your ear, my gentleman, my once-deceived. "A doctor of the psyche, I mean, about your delusion."

"I can see her as clearly as I can see that — " You search for words, and while your example is ungraceful, I applaud your effort to be frank. "As clearly as I can see that hat stand," you conclude, unable now to look my way.

She meets his glance.

"I think she's right," accords Bonecrust, pouring himself more of your treasured brandy. "Take a few weeks off and enjoy Lake Tahoe." He adds, brightly, "You can rent my cabin."

"Take all the time you need," she purrs.

Believe it to be true, my friend. She deceives you.

[4]

THE SLEEPING PILLS are many, and when they are all broken and stirred into the spirits-of-wine, they are a powerful poison.

Let self-murder be the farthest crime on your mind this night. Set your hand upon the phone.

"Professor Bonebeer," you are saying. "I think I may, actually. As you suggested. I need that rest, with a view of all that water."

You laugh, that plotter's chuckle I remember well, the way King Claudius laughed when he contemplated his forthcoming sins. But the way my lord Hamlet never did laugh. He laughed but little – he was never one to enjoy his own insight, but suffered it, as though to know so much was to live half-poisoned by the truth.

So, you are no Prince of Denmark. But neither was I destined to be queen. But wraith though I may be, I can nonetheless join lying lovers to their condign defeat.

"But you'll need to drop by with the key," you are saying. "And have a little more of my brandy."

We await his knock, you pacing unsure, I with unwavering sureness of the justice of his approaching sleep.

Quoth she, before you tumbled me,
You promised me to wed.

Did I not say that I could sing?

Ella and the Canary Prince

after "Cinderella"

FAIRY GODMOTHER was a chewed-looking thing, scaring me out of my skin every time she popped out of the privy with her "Anything you wish, my child." Bald and black-toothed, my first wish would be for a godmother a Christian could look upon and not faint.

She could be of some slight use from time to time. Once I allowed her to turn my cup of sack into sweet wine, and the taste was heavenly, except it turned to vinegar before five swallows. More a dust mop than a fairy, I finally asked her to stop visiting. "It's all very kind of you to grace our house, dear Godmother," I said politely enough, "but you're enough to curdle a mirror, need I elaborate?"

She put a curse on me: a plague should fall from Heaven, the wrath of every evil thing should flower on my body. I had a pimple on my cheek the next morning, and it faded by noon.

Rita let her help in the kitchen, toasting bread with a charm, shaking some of the wrinkles from the damask hunting scene with a malediction, but even Rita, plainer and more patient than I, had to ask her to please not come around here quite so often; she had a smell.

I will say that I am beautiful. My breakfast is a pullet's liver and one silver thimble of hock, no more. If a burgher pinches me I have the sense to slap his face, and sun never falls on this fair skin. Rita is the one no man would look at twice, freckled and brown-toothed.

She's a coarse thing, my natural sister, but with a laugh like music. Both of us are chaste, and when the boatmen sing their songs outside the city gates, we are ladies enough to blush.

But stepsister Ella was always hanging out the window when an entourage went by. Hanging out of her bodice — it was enough to make you cover your eyes or fall off your palfrey. And it was the year there was an entourage every other day, the King finally admitting to himself the Prince was one of those men who would rather play with canaries than hatch a son.

So Rita and I were stuck with a step-sibling who couldn't keep her lacings tied, and the King couldn't see a future for the kingdom he had bought from the Franks for as much as he could bleed from the populace.

It was a hard time. Snow during hay making, heat during Candlemas, and the ducks bald with blight. Ella would stand still wherever she was to watch the noblemen, plumed and silked, turning as they rode by to keep their eyes on her.

The King sent invitations across farm and waste. He threw everyone-comes-as-a-cat banquets. He threw everyone-comes-as-harlequins. He held stockings-cross-gartered balls and new-wine parties and then when no dainty was led forth beautiful enough to dazzle the Prince, the King threw a banquet so famous every rich noble maiden north of the Pyrenees showed up.

When all the cheese was carved from its wax and every barrel emptied to its lees, the King was left with a Prince going soft and unmarried, the wine steward fingering an empty purse.

The King had a habit of going in disguise among us. Dear soul, he fooled no one. "Here he comes," we'd nudge each other, a friar this time. Or, a ladies' maid, or a nun's priest or a prioress, one would almost say the King loved a disguise as much as a throne. And we'd all treat him with the offhand courtesy due to a serving wench, bestubbled under her rouge.

And one day it was I myself who said to this mock-vixen, "I don't know why the King, that wisest of men, doesn't do a cunning thing once before a plague flea bites him, Heaven forbid."

"And what wise thing would that be?" replied the fake flirt.

"I need not elaborate to you, my dear girl," I said, with a wee yawn, just enough to flare my nostrils prettily. "But if you were not a servant I'd say the King should seek underfoot what he prays from the sky."

Poor Highness, itching under his small clothes, distracted by the attentions of a miller, put his chin to mine and asked, "Meaning what, exactly?"

"Are there no beauties here in this very town to please the Prince?" I breathed.

Now this was when I was wearing my pearls, and had touched up my dimples with the olive pit ash. Let me say that I was as pretty as I needed to be.

The announcements were gaudy, hammered to the gates. A banquet for the daughters of the burghers and the gentlefolk alike, any comely maiden within walls was invited, and you can imagine the glee.

So we did corset ourselves, and dab paint, and pad out our God-given frontiers. Who could blame us? We suggested to Ella that if she would fetch a pan of water without stepping on the hem of her skirt, or slopping it all over the straw on the pantry floor, we would be happy to let her come, too.

I wanted Ella to come along. But she had wrestled herself into a bodice three sizes too small, and injured herself doing it.

"Poor Ella," I said, with some sincerity. "What a shame."

Rita and I went to the party and it was a crowd. More dye than in a tanner's vat, hair, eyebrows, and bleached-out wens, and powdered wrinkles. Any unwed woman with lungs and limbs was there, and beaming. And may I say that for once the beauty of my city melted me, how even the plainest of my fellow-ladies was a flower under the starry sky.

Of course Ella arrived, and I saw Godmother's handiwork at a glance, footmen with black, witless eyes, and a coach already starting to go yellow.

I groaned and wanted to warn Ella, and then when I saw her footwear I covered my eyes, embarrassed for her, because these were the poor, transparent slippers Godmother twice tried to offer me, riddled with bubbles, the effort of a glassmaker's apprentice.

Ella had such trouble with them, nailed to whatever spot she could find against a pillar by the pain of her feet, so when all the rest of the folk danced and curtseyed to the courtiers in attendance there was no one available to tour the breeding room but Ella.

Of course the footmen were rats. Of course the coach fell open, an orange gourd. And mice, everywhere, escaping the harness, such a headache.

When the time came, I didn't even bother. The red-knuckled King's men squeezed and fondled enough ankles trying on shoes to do the job three times over. You can't tell me it was all in the line of duty all that handling of arches and toes. And when at last they asked Rita, and Rita twisted her foot into a knob, trying to clench her toes, I gave up. Ella popped her foot into the discolored glass, and the wedding day was set.

Godmother showed up every morning for weeks, smiling with her nose in the air.

She expected me to feel slighted, or worse. Rita was offended, but I kept my peace. Finally Godmother asked me, peeking out from the chimney, upside down, "Aren't you angry, child? Aren't you furious at me?"

The King comes as a goose girl.

He comes as a juggler, hurt by lack of practice by his tumbling pins. He comes as a puppeteer, as a river merchant, as a dealer in dray mares. I let him in the servant's door, and all pretend that the secret is safe.

"Aren't you envious even a tiny bit?" asks Godmother. And to please and confound her I say "Yes." Because poor Ella waits for the Prince to come home from the yellow-finch mews, while I work with pleasure toward a throne as Ella's mother, superior in my mercy, her Queen.

Toad-Rich

I HAVE A MOUTH.

Some people have eyes, beauty, smarts – I've got a mouth.

Lydia my pretty sister has baby blues and walks around looking at the sky, the birds, wide-eyed and breathless. Dumb as my left tit but lovely, and when a knight-at-arms eases himself off his warhorse and steps into the shade, you could see him crane his neck to follow Lydia as she made her way out to the ducks.

Which is about all she was good for, domestic fowl, fed on old bread mixed with maize, the same stuff we set out for the geese. If a gosling chokes on a crust, it's one less for the weasels, is the way I looked at it. Lydia grew all tearful watching a duckling pump its neck, trying to not choke on a cob-butt, while I watched and laughed. That was about the only funny thing all day around here, barnyard fowl in fits.

Despite what you might think we got along pretty well. I handled the thinking for Mama and Lydia, and I bred those hounds you've heard of, eyes like weep-holes but capable of following a vixen from here to Sodom. The approach I took was: drown the runts, keep the stud hounds full of fresh meat, and don't be too fussy what kind: duck, goose, mutt. I kept the bitches in heat feeding them wither-wort and musk-of-rut I boiled down to a paste. They whelped until they staggered.

Then I axed them, chopped them up, and kept the kennel fat. Courtiers cantered up from all directions fingering their florins. I weighed my apron down with gold some summer days, no silver here, only the finest coin. I kept the prices up by thinning out the yappers.

ONE DAY a dog bit my shank, a little nip, and it went puffy. I had to stay indoors, watching the progress of the duck parade sister Lyd led from pond to pen. The sight warmed my heart, my guileless sibling, marching with her birds. I cooked a poultice with Mama's help, and thonged it onto my lame limb.

I called for Lydia. "Take the buckets," I said, "and fetch some water from the well, and don't stand around blinking at the serving lads on the path. Go there, come back, and get back to your sewing." I had to blush, ordering Lydia around this way, but it was an iron habit.

Lyd curtseyed, kind to me, no matter what, and Mama stared at both of us like a woman cursed with knowledge of the past and present. She didn't hate life, but gave that impression, stony faced and hard – brave men looked away when she entered a room. But Mama and I share a humor, granite on the outside, almost human in the heart.

Truth to tell, I do indulge a weakness, and sometimes stroke a pup or let a brood bitch take a morsel from my hand. When no one's looking. And I confess to a fondness for Mama and my sister Lyd. I can't resist this tender feeling, almost foreign to my soul.

THAT TERRIBLE MORNING Lydia ran back panting, out of breath, bodice laces bursting. She couldn't speak at first.

The pinkness was subsiding from my bite and I was feeling half happy with the world.

"Becky!" cried Lydia at last. "Mama!" Each familiar syllable sounding like a burp, glittering cough-up flying through the air to our feet, two jewels. Topaz and a ruby, well-set and fine.

Lydia puked out her tale, an emerald for each noun, a diamond for each verb, and when she coughed, pure gold. Painful and frightening both, and yet by the end of her narration a little mountain of treasure glittered on the straw.

"Dear Lydia," I said, caressing her. "Such a trial." All I could think was: who did this to poor Lyd? Only half-believing her tale. No old woman waits at wells in this county, not if she knows what's smart. You find your way to the wellhead fast and nimbly. The last old woman who loitered was the one who had an infant just fallen in, bawling for her baby. The woman was twenty years past childbearing, a freakish thing. We burned her.

We don't tarry at anything in this part of God's earth, and we don't say good day, or fair-thee-well. We use our mouths for telling people what we think of them, and as a result a nice silence is all we hear from Sunday till Christmas. Someone wears a new stocking, or sings a new song, we step right up and tell him the one he wore last year was better, and too bad his voice is as ugly as his face.

So it wasn't a desire to be a bijoux spewer that flounced me out into the lane, all skirt and bad leg. I was looking out for the virtue of the countryside, and ready to find this stranger who had nothing better to do than blast an innocent and witless girl with an affliction.

I was hunting for the wayfarer who had harmed my sister.

There was no one at the well. One or two goodwives peeped out of the hedging, saw it was me and peeped back in again. I dropped the buckets one by one — for in her frightened haste Lydia had neglected her duty — when this witch dragged herself, all wens and gums, right up to where I sweated, hauling a billy goat skin full of well water from the very bottom of the hole.

"Give me but a drink, good lass," said this insult to appearance, this counter to the faith that God is imaged in the human form.

I had heard Lydia's gold-throttled recitation of this greeting, but couldn't help but maintain the standards of our town. "Call that a face, dear friend?" I responded. "Call that a way of making way upon the summer landscape, grinning like a wound, squinting like a pig's sphincter? Let me favor you with an honest piece of advice — "

I coughed.

Just a frog in my throat, I reckoned, hawking, spitting out a toad, glistening with my saliva and quite satisfied to belly-down, solemn as Solomon, right there in the mud, blink, blink.

"The water you need's for bathing," I belched, uttering a lizard, two snakes, and a moth.

The old woman grinned.

"I'll skin you to the bone," I said, seizing her bony frame, cloak and gristle. Spiders scurried down my chin. "I'll have you flogged!" I cried, crickets scuttling to the dust. "You'll be pilloried in the market until All Saints'," I added, each word the eruption of a worm.

But then I remembered my manners, the tradition of honesty and good faith that makes our town renowned, frankness and outspokenness our pride. No longer would I dally with this hag. I strangled her with the well rope, then and there, cursing bugs into her face.

There were weeks of fury, ruined sleep, bitterness. Mama swept larvae, daddy longlegs, thrips, and patiently shoveled garnets, opals, cameos, rings. I endured an era of unhappiness. I felt sorry for myself, and wept myself dry of tears.

One morning a prince rode into the barnyard, tickled by rumor into soft words, kissing poor Lydia's hand. And taking it in marriage. "And the two of you as welcome guests," smiled the prince, all teeth, cheek, and chin.

The wedding was celebrated three long nights, all Lydia-produced gold and tiaras, even on the serving wenches. Mama went perfumed and dimpled, a new woman. I attended veiled, silent as a nun.

All so just, the goodwives whispered. The one with the mouth cursed, the demure and kindly blessed and honored.

But then the whispers changed.

Merchants rumored the infamy, from lake to sea, the beautiful, weak-minded Lydia, kept by a king's son in a tower. Stewards pinched her into utterance when inspiration failed. She gasped out even more brilliant gems, now, pearls and amber, and all but worthless.

Worse than worthless. You've heard how these days diamonds are used as gizzard stones for geese, how gold is melted into leading for the spires. You've heard how silver is nailed into boot heels. Rubies are ground for sandpaper. Opals are employed as sling stones. Some byways drift with topaz, others are cobbled with sapphire. All because poor Lydia whispers her prayers each night, more gems by the bushel basket, a countinghouse rendered worthless by sheer glut. Her groom the prince despairs, the shadow of a man.

While I no longer weep. I have sold off the last of my pups, and tend a lowlier, more exotic breed. The midge and the silverfish I pinch and rinse from my fingers. The common tadpole I feed to the viper, the salamanders to the asp. I cull my tribe of scuttlebugs and wasps, drowning, burning, thrashing lifeless all but the beautiful, all but the rare.

It takes time, but I have enough of that.

I do a fruitful, thriving business in pilgrims, in errant squires, in knights bound for the Holy Sepulcher. My banners flutter in the breeze: This way to the adder, Cleopatra's bane. This way to the serpent, scourge of Eden. This way to the silk moth, prize of the east – watch him feed, watch him weave, watch him sleep.

Friars queue, ambassadors jostle. Tinkers bribe their way to the head of the line. Mama guides them from pen to cage, showing off poison spiders for the spiteful, butterflies for the betrothed, scarabs and centipedes for the curious, all marvelous, all rare.

Mama and I will buy Lydia back with a dragonfly, and a wasp's nest. The prince will sell her for any price, snails, snakeskin, moth-glitter, poison-arrow toad. If that fails, then with a bee swarm, wax, and apple-blossom honey. The sphinx moth, the chameleon, the bat-wing. Each more precious than a gem.

We bolt our windows nightly against potential dragonfly thieves, armed with clubs of gold. Highwaymen brood with emerald dirks, and children skim silver plates across the pond. No living thing is too small or common – lizard's kid or circus flea – and no vermin is without wonder, even so lowly a creature as myself, rich in love and toads.

The Flounder's Kiss

after "The Fisherman and his Wife"

MY BEAUTIFUL BRIDE said if you spend all your time fishing the river you catch nothing but monkfish and bream. You get water wens all over your feet. If you want money, she said, you go sea fishing.

So there I was, a river man all my life, marrying after I had nine gray hairs, pricing fisher's small-craft at the weekly sale. Most of those belly-up clinker-builts belong to dead fishermen, their bodies feeding crabs, and everybody knows it. It keeps the prices down, but I decided to be a beach fisher, and I had some luck.

You have to take the long view. You like whelks, you eat whelks. Shellfish don't bother me. When I don't catch anything, the tide all the way to the sunken merchantman in the mouth of Zeebrugge harbor, I trudge back and start clamming. Eight, nine clams and you have supper.

Yanni, my rose-cheeked wife, would say, "All day out there and you come home with what?" That lovely mouth of hers, working nonstop.

"I have six fine cockles," I would answer.

Or, if the tide had run well, two fine whiting. Or two soles, or a John Dory, or a dozen pier mussels. Whatever it was, and they were always prime. I don't want to eat anything diseased or deformed or that looks peculiar.

The fact is that some days I can't bring myself to eat fish. It's not just that fish flop around with their mouths open. They have slits they breathe through and eyes that look up like pennies, and there's nothing you can do to tell a fish to lie still. You can use one of those mallets especially made for shutting fish up, "head hammers," the dory men around here call them in their usual pithy, jocular way, but about the only thing you can say to a fish is nothing.

Tourists love it. We put on these wooden mud-treaders, and you can hear them calling to their kids, "Look, how darling, wooden shoes." And I, for one, always wave and smile. I know they can't help it, so far from home and nothing to look at but a man going to work with about twenty ells of net on his back.

"You bother to catch one pilchard, Weebs, you might as well catch a hundred," my wife would say. Always sewing, needle winking up and down. Skirts, blouses, collars, gloves. "I might as well be a herring gull you come back with such tiny little fish."

"It takes a lot to maneuver the net with just two arms," I would reply. "You need a strong back and a feel for the current."

"You've got talent, Weebs," she would respond. "A rare genius. You ought to win a prize for being able to work for less money than anyone who ever scraped mud."

"You want me to catch flounder."

"Eels," Yanni would reply, squinting at her needle.

"Eels have two hearts," I would say. "They crawl over land. They have conventions in the ocean, they have nests in the hills. An eel is too complicated to eat. I like pilchards. You can hold a fish like that in your hand."

"Men," my wife would say.

"There's something about a herring that says I'm made for eating, it's okay to eat me, I have an eye on each side of my head and I am going to be eaten by something I never saw coming, it might as well be you."

"Catch something worth the effort," she would reply. Bored, having given up on me. But still talking about it, one of those people who can't shut up. She would walk into a room making announcements saying she was cold, I would be late for high tide, why was it so dark, where was her darning.

It was a glorious day for watching clouds. I had caught nothing. The sea was filthy, a gale out of the northwest. All the horsefishers were in their stables. The sailorfishers were sipping juniper spirits by their fires, and there was only I myself, on the broad flat beach. I didn't want to come home wet with rain and wet with brine, blue and nothing to show for it but a pocketful of limpets.

You cast your net, and it looks pretty, black lace spreading out. When it drifts down over the water there is a splash where the netting settles, and the sound of it is what satisfies. Casting the net, you feel the waves calm under the span you mended and sometimes I could do it well into the dark, regardless whether or not I caught a fingerling.

I was almost ready to quit for the night. One more cast, I told myself. Just one more. It's a serene sight, the net sweeping up, hanging over the water, lifting with the wind. The net drifted onto the sea. And it happened. The net tugged, tightened. And there it was as I hauled in the net, the famous fish, the size of a Michaelmas tureen, fat and silver.

I have a great aversion to flounders. I can't stand to take them by the tail, much less slit one open. They have their eyes close together on one side of their head, and they swim around blind on one side, looking up at the sky with the other. I want something simple to eat, not a living curiosity.

I realized, however, that it was worth a guilder or two, a fish like this, an armload, and while I am not the most gifted fisherman alive I am no fool. I pulled the one-sided creature out as it flopped in the net. I dragged it onto the beach, and untangled the net, and then I heard something. I looked up, looked around, my head tilting this way and that. The wind was whistling, and I was not sure what I heard.

Maybe it was a tourist talking, one of the day-trip spinsters out of Southampton; they ferry across and flirt at a distance. They say things like "What a wonderful fish you have just caught," in German, as though I would ever speak a syllable of the language. The tourists are the equivalent of herring themselves, the poor dears. It would be just like one to be chattering in a rising wind in the dusk in the middle of nowhere. Not just talking, arguing, jabbering to make a point.

I stooped to gather in enough fish to buy a silver thimble and a bolt of silk when I realized that the muttering was close to my ear. I dropped the flounder. It smacked the sand and made that shrugging flopping I hate in fish – why can't they just fall asleep and die? The fish said clearly, but in a small voice, "Wish. Go ahead wish. Just wish. Any wish. Don't wait – wish."

I seized my gutting knife and just about used it, out of horror. But instead I asked it a question.

I did feel strange as I spoke. My brother shovels waffles into the oven on a paddle and has a cellar of cheese. My sister married a brewer, beer and fat children. My father took tolls on a bridge with carved seraphim and saints, burghers and fair ladies and military men calling him by name, wishing him well.

And I was talking to a fish.

And, even worse, that very fish was talking right back. "Any wish. Then let me go."

It was persistent, this idiot babble flowing from the fish. So I made a wish. I asked for a bucket full of herring, pink-gilled, enough for tonight and a few left over for the market.

BY CANDLELIGHT Yanni picked a spine-bone from her mouth and said, her eyebrows up, not wanting to admit it, "That was most delicious, Weebs. Most tasty little fish I have ever supped upon."

"There's a story behind that fish," I said.

She gave me one of her bedroom glances, dabbed her pretty lips.

"But never mind," I said.

"Tell me," she said.

I pushed my plate away, put my elbows on my table, and took a sip of beer, dark brew, tart, almost like vinegar. I smiled. I said, "You won't believe it."

Not a quarter of an hour later I was wading into the surf. "Fish!" I called. "Big fish! Flounder!"

It was raining hard. Despite what you might have heard, there was no poem, no song. There was a lump on my head, and one eye was swelling shut. I bellowed into the wind, now straight out of the north.

"One more boon," I asked.

Waves broke over me, drowning the sound of my voice. There were no fish. The fish were vanished from the sea. I stood drenched, about to turn away, when the fish was there at my side, its eyes two peas side by side.

"One more!" I said. I was standing in a storm talking to a fish, and before shame or common sense could silence me I repeated Yanni's desire.

I hurried back, running along the dike. Cows with their big, white foreheads stared at me from within their mangers, and when I half-collapsed in my cottage she seized me by my jerkin and turned me around. "Look!"

The kettle had unbent its hook, fallen into the fire, solid gold and impossible to drag out of the embers. "It's going to melt!" she cried.

"You wanted it turned to gold," I said.

"Go back and get this made into money."

I panted, dripping, catching my breath. "Money?"

"Coins! Sovereigns, ducats, dollars. We can't do anything with this."

"It's beautiful!"

"And then ask for brains, Weebs. For you. For inside your head."

"You should try to be more patient, dear Yanni," I said. I think it was the only time I had ever offered her such advice.

She put her hands on her hips. In her apron and her cap she told me what she thought of me. All this time I had thought her pensive, moody, emotional. But I thought she loved me.

I took my time. The wind was warm, out of the west now, and there were a few stars. When I was a boy I would want to stand outside in the wind and feel my sweater and my sleeves billow and flow, flying. Both feet on the ground, but flying in my heart.

"Fish! Magic flounder!"

It must have known. Once it began to trade in human desire it was finished. No net is worse. It nosed upward, out of the waves. Why it even listened I cannot guess. I thrust my hand into a gill, seized a fin, and hauled the creature with all my strength. I dragged it up where the sand was dry, black reeds, gulls stirring, croaking.

The fish was talking nonstop. I tugged my knife free of the belt and cut the flounder, gills to tail, and emptied him out on the sand.

THERE HAS BEEN some question about my wife. Some say the fish renounced the boons, took it all back, and sent us into poverty. Some say my wife left me, taking the golden kettle with her, swinging it by one fist, strong as she was famous to be.

Proof against this is the kettle I still possess, heavy as an anvil, chipped at slowly over the years, shavings of pure gold to buy feather quilts and heifers. And this is not the only precious metal in my house. A golden pendant the shape of a woman's mouth dangles ever at my breast.

A parting gift? some ask.

Or a replacement for her, suggests the even-smarter guest with a chuckle, enjoying my roast goose.

Fish do not die quickly. They take their time. And even a magic fish is slow to understand. Give me silence, I wished, crouching over him, knife in hand. Silence, and the power to bring her back some day, should it please me, one kiss upon her golden lips.

Bite the Hand

THE CUSTOMS DECLARATION attached to the large package read: mummified specimen.

What are our border officials doing, allowing shriveled nightmares into the land of the free, I wanted to ask. Raymond had heard the delivery truck, and was dashing down the stairs.

Weren't you afraid, living with such strange relics, my current gentleman friend inquires, and I smile, in my special way, and allow that I'm afraid of nothing.

"It's here at last!" Raymond cried, reading the shipping label.

Professors have a good deal of idle time on their hands, and they get paid well, with plenty of time for expensive and pointless behavior. Raymond scurried and got his pocketknife, and then ran to get his claw hammer and his screwdriver, and at last had to get the crowbar from the garage. "I've always dreamed of owning one of these!" he exclaimed. "Oh, this is a wonder indeed!"

He even talked like a book.

It was half-horse, half-man, no question. A centaur, found by one of the curiosity merchants Raymond e-mails, "the last one of its kind."

Raymond had to see the desiccated mannikin mounted in a bell jar, so the department chairperson and visiting scholars could peer at it and say, "I thought they were mythical" during brunch the following Sunday.

Both man-front and horse-rear were midget. The medical school sent its department vice-director over to look for sutures and telltale joiner's glue, but this was real, a man's upper body and a stallion's nether, and all I could keep murmuring was, "Isn't it a marvel?"

After the caterer's minions cleaned up the quiche and bubbly, I kept putting the thing back onto the shelf with the plaster cast of Big Foot's private parts, found in a mud wallow near Mount Shasta, always a distress to me whenever I happen upon it. But Raymond got that stubborn little Mount Rushmore expression on his face, and said, "Leave it where we can see it."

It was in the local newspaper that week, *English Prof Bags Horse-man*, and there was Raymond's face, looking very much the Andrew Marvell scholar, his smile gracing the *Elm Hill News Press* and proving that at least one member of the ivory tower set had world enough and time to add to his collection of "oddities from around the globe."

This was just one more, to go along with the balding unicorn, with that suspicious seam twixt horn and head, and that mummified elf, looking very much like the permanent unborn human. Raymond was a man who fed his pet lorikeets pistachio nuts, handfuls of them while the yellow and lime-green charmers hopped all over him, imitating his gentle voice, "Sweet little darlings," a hopeless fool through and through. Women found him endlessly forgivable, regardless of his gaffes and whimsies.

I know how to survive married life: you keep your mouth shut, smile, and bide your time. My plan was to fake a burglary, snap up some insurance money, and eventually have a nice three-story Victorian a woman could live in without listening to English department gossip every night.

The afternoon the housekeeper complained it took me awhile to understand the enormity, as my Mom used to say.

"It moved!" Dora said, all hips and breasts, and I wondered if Raymond had dropped home early and slipped back into one of his old regrettable habits, like the sort that caused all that misunderstanding outside the ladies' room in the city park.

"It moved!" repeated Dora, a tireless woman of Norwegian descent, always reporting to me what she watched on TV the night before. "The centaur wiggled!" she exclaimed.

Raymond had once commented that Dora smelled of marijuana, and I took note that Raymond had gotten close enough to scent Dora's personal odor, whatever it might be.

Furthermore, it sounded as though Dora had said that the *center* wiggled, and I put down my teacup in a mood of confused despair. "At me!" she added, and I took a moment to consider my life, how my late mother had warned me against marrying a nervous academic. "His head is in the clouds," she had opined, a woman who had run a shipping company after a load of kapok fell out of the boxcar suffocating Dad.

Raymond is handsome in a careless way, nice eyebrows, broad shoulders. He had not wanted children, and neither had I, but he had his birds and his stuffed were-pig and his satyr's hoof instead. I had nothing but Raymond, a man who got excited reading bone catalogs.

"What has he done?" I asked, meaning: I would divorce the neurasthenic freak at last.

"I was dusting it with the duster," Dora said, hand to breast. "And it bit me!"

I marched down the hall, and there was the centaur, half-human, half-pony, looking stiff and still. "What happened to the glass covering?" I asked. The bell jar had vanished, and Dora explained that the "little guy" had looked in need of a whisk with the ostrich feathers.

I gave the withered horror a closer examination, and he did look a little dusty in the crevices, especially down around his private regions. So I borrowed a dust cloth from Dora, gave the little fellow's face and other areas a gentle wipe, and he bit me, too. A nip, right on my knuckle.

I was stunned.

And before I knew what I was doing, I hit back.

"It was suspended animation," Dora was saying as I realized what I had done. She has tapes of *Nova* going back ten years. She knows all about galaxies at the edge of the universe, cloned goats, psychic experiments. "It wasn't really dead!" she said. "Only suspended!"

Red blood on my hands, I fired Dora, and then when Dora insisted that she would sue me for violating a verbal contract, I hired her back again, on condition that she would resuscitate the bloody man-half on the floor.

Dora gave the gory little grotesque the kiss of life, but it didn't work. She kept looking up with a small smear of blood on her mouth, saying "You killed him! It's murder, Mrs. Quince."

"Self-defense," I said.

"He was just coming back to life after an eon," said Dora.

I considered my position.

"He was warmed by human contact," Dora was saying, "and you — "

I know how to survive married life, and I know how to manage a reversal. I crumpled up my face, and wept.

Dora put her arm around me, walked me down the stairs, saying that she had spoken too abruptly, "We should always count to ten when we are mad," she said.

Raymond popped home from his graduate seminar on the cavalier poets just then, brim full of the latest news on metaphor. He caught one look at my tearstained face, and Dora's near-swoon of consolation, and dropped his backpack full of quarterlies.

"Dora wrecked the centaur," I said, talking fast. "She broke its neck — we mustn't fire Dora because she has two kids in junior high but we should insist she have treatment for her problem."

Dora took in a sharp breath, but her words stuck.

Raymond took one look at the remains of the centaur, and he was speechless with anguish. I failed to see the point of all his sorrow. It was dead now, and it had been dead when he ordered it from Brussels, except that it had not been absolutely deceased in the strictest sense.

"Blood, flowed from its flesh," he said at last. "Like a living thing."

No ordeal is so crushing that it cannot be finessed. Even the load of kapok that fell upon my dad could have been survived by a man less afraid of closed-in places.

"It was imperfectly mummified," I said. "Send it back."

"It moved its head and looked at me," Dora insisted.

I raised one eyebrow, in my special way.

DORA FELL into heavier and heavier dependencies on whatever drugs are in fashion. She took to accusing me of cruelty in letters to the *Elm Hill News Press*, the editor of which has become a kind and well-spoken gentleman friend of mine. She took to writing long declarations of love to Raymond, portions of which he quotes to his graduate seminar as examples of hyperbole. And when Dora gets out of the medical center she will move to Florida with her two foster-home-addled teens.

Raymond has agreed to an amicable divorce, and has moved to a double-wide trailer at the edge of the reservoir. He says that living alone has its good points. He has even sworn off his fondness for collecting, after the newspaper ran an article describing each and every one of his curiosities as frauds.

"How could they know?" Raymond was moaning, the last time he dropped by to pick up his junk mail. "Where did they obtain all their information?"

He has sold off his treasures, each collectible grotesque.

All but one – which he could not find.

This house is lovely, and I enjoy the quiet. I stay in bed late, and take tea by the bay window, watching the sun through the elms and the sycamores. If only I could sleep better at night, and did not have dreams.

I wake alone, and sit bolt up in the broad, cold bed. I do not utter a word, knowing how futile speech can often be, and every night I wake to a sound down the corridors through the dark, the constant music of hooves.

Daphne

YOU KNOW HOW THE SUN IS, how he won't shut up on one of those dry, drought-golden days, the vineyards blue-black with fruit, the oxcarts groaning by, every human being wishing for a portion of shade.

Apollo, the sun god, was what you would expect – all smiles, all mouth, too beautiful to look at, and knowing it. Oh, he was good company, dropping by the fields where honest women were herding geese or cranking buckets out of the well, and he'd speak in that voice that was like the sky itself favoring you with its attention.

I had a simple life. My own father was the river god Peneus, and my mother was a former village maiden who, taking her ease by river bathing a hot late summer afternoon, felt the lap and sinew of my father around, beneath, within. Rivers are promiscuous, ardent, and deep. My mother spent years pensive, alone, but sustained by the knowledge that she had once been loved. She raised me to make straw dolls and wax horses, all the petty, pretty toys of girlhood, but never let me forget that I was the daughter of the river – that distant father who never addresses his children but is, at the same time, always faithful to them.

The sun god would amble by and flirt, but I paid him no attention. Young mortal men would come around, too, all blushes and stammers, and I would shake my head and tell them that the wedding candle and the bridal bed held no magic for me. The daughter of the deep current has no great fondness for the merely human breath of any lover, and the prospect of becoming a wife filled me with no happiness.

One day I waded into the river.

I let the current surround and know me. The coursing, seaward longing of my father for the deeper ocean was always his great failing, and his lasting strength. My father pulsed all around my body, both on his way to the salt ocean and steadily in one place at the same time.

"Hear me," I whispered.

I heard no answer.

"Oh father, listen to me," I prayed.

The ripples of river water glittered.

I said, "Make me a virgin all my years – make me one who does not tarry with mankind."

And my father spoke at last, in that water-lunged, rotund whisper. You've heard my father speak, soft syllables among the willow branches, muttering whispers in the shadow of the bridge. "Will I not have grandchildren?" he complained. "No little ones, splashing along my banks?"

I begged him again to bless my maidenhead, and told him that just as Diana the Huntress Immortal was no lover of men, so I, too, would seek a chaste existence. I would enjoy a noble life worthy, after all, of the river's daughter.

This last argument teased the concession from him. The river god is powerful, with his long, grappling arms full-muscled each spring, when the mountains are dark with rain. But the river god is not so mighty he does not feel the weight of the even greater gods, the powerful sea in his abyss, the sun with his yodeling, arrogant look-at-me each day. So with a reluctant, but not unkind sigh, he blessed my virginity, and with a loving, guarded murmur added, "Be kind to your mother, Daphne – I still hold her in my heart."

My father – constant, stubborn, fickle, undying. And you ask why I wanted nothing to do with mortal men.

It was not very long before the god Apollo came around as usual, parting the wheat field with his athletic stride, laughing. Tossing back his head and laughing – the god was one great, life-consuming laugh.

But on this day he did not pass me by. Something about me had changed. Perhaps my private vow had altered me, and increased my beauty. The sky was not enough for him, he swore – he desired me.

"Daphne," he said, "let's go see the berries ripen on the bush."

I did not meet his gaze.

"Let's go watch the olive branches get heavy with their bounty," he added, and other such things, all god-chat meaning: let me play in-and-out with you over on the hillside, my dear, and I'll leave you alone and forsaken ever after.

I told him I had taken a vow of chastity.

He frowned as he smiled. "As a divinity, I can dismiss this vow," he said, all teeth and sparkle.

I made no further reply.

"Oh, Daphne, have you not dreamed of being the mother of the sun god's brood?" he asked.

I had nothing to say.

The god would not shut up. He came to see me for days. Each morning he would split the hillsides with his beaming countenance, and each noon he would lay his hot, huge hands all over my body as I carried the bucket from the well, reaching down and feeling me where ever he could, shoulders, brow. But I would not allow him the private favors he sought.

I HEARD HIM on his way toward me that hot day. He was even more merry than ever. He talked as he came along the wending road from the village, as I was out collecting thyme for my mother's stew.

"Wouldn't that head look fine bedecked with a crown?" he sang. "Wouldn't that pair of hips look just right, graced with the girdle of a queen and the silks of a monarch, my comely bride? Wouldn't those lips come alive under the — "

But I had heard enough, and casting the sweet-scented herbs to the ground, I walked away. I walked fast.

I hurried.

He followed, never ceasing to talk, his unending spiel enough to wither crops. He described how passionate he had always proved as a lover, how the hills stirred and brought forth forests at his caress, how poppies broke into blossom at his breath.

And who was I? he asked.

Who was I? he said again, beginning to grow surly. Who was I, a mere river-godkin's daughter, to turn aside the love of the father of so much life, and a well-favored, rich-voiced Dad of All at that.

Right then I made my terrible error.

I made my mortal blunder.

I began to run.

As I ran, Apollo strode along with me, faster than any greyhound panting after his hare. He circled me as I fled, bounded along, crossed my path, back and forth, mocking, seeking, all but capturing me against my will, as though pursuit made his lust all the keener. In my ignorant virginity I began to weep, my next mistake. Because my wet tears merely made him laugh.

I ran as no woman has ever run, fled as few mortals have ever flown, down the slope of the river valley, the sun god matching me stride for stride, his sky-warm breath at my shoulder. I reached the side of the river, and called out just as he seized me.

He was very strong.

My voice swept linnets from the willows. It startled harvest mice in their slumber. Help me, Father. I heard the god of the sun chuckle at my ear. He said, "What can a mere water godlet do to keep my lust at bay?"

My father did not forget me.

My fingers split. My arms throbbed, and broke wide open. Working fibers snaked down the veins of my lungs. My feet seized and held the bank of the river, a root from my spine to the soil, and down, into the cold stone. Wide into the sky I held my beseeching arms. They branched, and my full-leafed embrace filled the blue from where I panted, a green-pithed tree, rooted to the earth.

Well Apollo loved me then, weeping, feeling the trilling of my human heart within my wooden girth. Because the gods love mortals. They seek our beauty, our courage, our joy. They envy us our hope. We are in our hearts what they can never master, and all the night long the lord of light keened beside me, weeping for the love he would never win.

To this day when a daphne blossoms, or when any tree breaks

into leaf, you can feel how the sun is chastened, faithful to the living he can worship but never possess. And as for me — feel no sorrow. When you see the wind stir the greenwood, or when you turn the pages of a book made from a tree's still-blameless flesh, lean close and listen.

You hear my voice.

Naked Little Men

after "The Shoemaker and the Elves"

HANS WAS A COMPLAINER. He came from a country of complainers, tree country, you can't find people except by following the far-off sounds of complaints drifting through the woods. You get there, and feasting's in progress, huge cheeses and jugs of beer, fat, red-cheeked folk, all complaining.

Where's the shade. How many do you have, I don't have half as many. Why wasn't it this warm last year. Look at her face and then look at mine. Nonstop. I was always pleasant, even joined in a little, there was always a little skin on the cream or bubbles in the gouda, something, but you had to be inventive — things were close to perfect except for the sour expressions of the Complaint-folk.

My husband even sang songs that complained, rhymes about how terrible it was in the wind and in the sun and in night and day, how awful it was. He was a man who wouldn't hang cobbler on his eave it had to be shoemaker, wanting the silk-gown trade to walk in and see him sitting there complaining why the light wasn't any better or when it was going to stop raining or why I wouldn't answer him when he called me, as though I had nothing better to do. Wondering where the trade was, pricking his finger every time he looked up to squint at the door.

While Hans was complaining he was looking, and when he looked he saw his new wife and his hides on the table and out the doorway a goose and a puddle and a pasture with three cows. When he looked out the window he saw a puddle and a bucket. And trees. He saw trees, trees everywhere, leaves, branches, moss, bark.

Not one of the trees with a foot needing a sole. He'd rub tallow on the hinges of the shoemaker sign so it didn't creak, he saw a new load of hides arriving, the carter griping about how far it was all the way out here, it would be triple the price next time, he had no idea, a city man taking up one of the local habits.

A city woman myself I've never been good at it. I can't help it, I have a kindly nature and "Good morning" comes out of my mouth quicker than "What are *you* looking at?"

"Shoemaker to the Trees" I used to call him and he would make one of his bird-like laughs, because we did have a cozy time or two, me showing him to wrestle a cutpurse to the ground and hurting his back that time, not my fault he's a slip of a man and my mother gave birth to a crop of daughters made to lift and carry.

But when we moved to town he wanted a house all eaves, with shoemaker hanging off each one of them, and down by the market, too, costing half a year's goose throttling just to pay the landlord to let us have the place three months and would he please take the pigs out of the back, we'd thought of sleeping there, the loft full of hides.

So there we were, and Hans complaining just as well as ever, the song about the blue sky so bare it made him empty, and the one about how the bones in his body made him think of bones, all the old tree-country songs, and I just let him sing, quiet-like.

City people like me can open a door and we can shut it, I always say, meaning we can close a mouth when we have to.

But it was a terrible thing, that winter. Not to lift my voice now in sorrow or self-pity, but the chickens froze hard on the slate roofs and the pigeons drifted in the wind, little feet sticking up so you could pick them up, squabs flat on one side roasting just as well as the rounded ones used to.

But soon there weren't any bones in the street, not for dog or man, and the grain we got in the sacks was sprouted and dead already, in a hurry, one year come and gone in the opinion of this particular barley. We had sackcloth bread. We had street gleaning bread. We had spit and cold air bread, until my husband traded all his hides for a cheese knob and a jar of mustard, the poor fool.

We went to bed with a scrap of leather left on the bench, yellow skin fit for one shoe, maybe two if the hand that stitched it stretched as it stitched. And not a country bench, either, one of the new city benches, ash and yew and neat's foot rubbed to a color you'd call pretty if you didn't know it cost the tanned suits of two bullocks just to get it in the door, three to get it pegged together, plus a loaf to the carriers for their pains.

Hungry? Not a bit. Hunger had been nine weeks ago, when we were eating stick-shaving soap. Hunger had been ten weeks past when we were chewing cat's gristle and calling it sweet.

Hunger would come if we had sat and eaten four days, hour after hour, until we awoke to the beginning of what a normal healthy human being would have started to feel an inkling of. Which would have been hunger.

And cold. Husband like an iron chair in my arms, don't ask about the cold. If it had been cold we would have been roiling in our sweat. Cold would have had us sunning in our small-clothes. Cold. A fire crackling and all the chinks stopped, heated up for days we would have ascended to the level we could start to shiver, the shivering long since frozen from our bones.

We slept. Morning when I could open my eyes there he was, a husband driven mad, hunger mad, bleak-winter-sun and empty-future mad, laughing and dancing and all I could think was where the priest was, who was big enough to wrestle a devil out of a man, was he still living or had he died, too, of the frost and sleeping in the church under a slab.

So I had to pick my husband up myself, and give him a little shake, and when he woke he was laughing again, saying, "The shoes! The shoes!" Poor man, the last word he knew.

When I went into the shop there was a pair. Lovely, and neat-stitched, not a slip. The sole fine-wrought, Flemish-fit, we call it, the craft most shoemakers skip, mine included, costing too much time. The collar, the tongue, the buckle, all the breath-smooth work you can imagine, and balanced in the hand.

I WAS AFRAID, ACTUALLY. Worried.

What happens when the wonderful happens is you think: wait, who did this, and why. My husband attested that he didn't do it, and didn't know who did.

We sold it to the first man in, a silk-capped traveler — a cur had torn his boot, and he went from surly to smiles in a trice. He slipped them on, and marched away, leaving my palm weighted with gold coin.

Forgive the details, the glee, the happy embrace, because we had our joy, the slip of a man and I. The scurrying about, the hides, the bench, the few stitches started, the cabbage and eel, the cakes and sow's cheeks so much after fasting. Sleep was all we hungered for by dark.

And next morning, half-hoping, it was too much to dream. There was a shop full of boots, of slippers, ladies' and ladies' maids and gentleman's guards, and children's first-soles, and all of it matchless. And customers to follow, a shop full of dazzled, top-price-paying souls.

It was my way. It was. A city woman, I know what is called for, a thanks to the benefactor, return a smile with smiling. Not for me the country manner, trading a curse for a greeting, a fist for a wave.

"Let us see who does this," I said. And thank them well. Just tonight, hide and look.

Little knot of a man, trembling, big-eyed, he finally agreed. And lurking in the feed-shelves, hunched up, we saw.

Some wonder and want to know. Some ask what we saw. "Oh, tell!" they say.

NAKED LITTLE MEN.

A shock, needless to describe. Such a sight, the creatures, built as men are, town and field, but shameless. You could see their all, but not their fingers, so fast they were a twinkle of needle, a blur of thread shot through leather, so quick that in the time a man would take to clear his throat a sole would be attached.

"Tonight we'll thank them," I said when we were alone.

Linen is made for my hands. Flax grows looking forward to my needle. What a little naked man can do with thread and leather I can with needle and a cloth, though slow, being human and far from small.

These were breeches and blouses for a king's courtiers, matching, Lincoln-green, and caps to fit, the suits for gentlemen, if gentle people came as big as cats.

The shoemaker said what they needed was a good cursing, a man to say, "Who asked you to sit on my bench?" He said we should act angry so they'd come back out of spite, just to bother. They did have little laughs, like blades through kidskin, not music, I can tell you. Or ignore them, he said, let them think we tolerated their handicraft, not that we depended on it.

The story goes around that the naked little men put on the clothes, found them delightful, sang a song, danced, and left us to our lives and to ensuing greater happiness.

I am proud, but no more than is required to learn from a night's events. What took place defies faith. The naked little men seized the clothes and laughed, but it was not the sort of laughter that engages. Hand to mouth and holding breath I saw them mock my efforts, trousers on their heads, sleeves up one leg, and excited in ways I will not describe except to refer to barnyard scenes.

They left us to our winter, which was far from done.

My husband makes do. His reputation is enough to carry him, although talk is that he has slipped a little in his craft, they say it's the volume of trade he does now, two apprentices and a wife who lets the porridge cool before she calls him.

My private hope is my husband will complain again some day. That he will say how terrible it is that walls and roofs and land and folk are around at all just to vex him.

My faith is he'll sing the song about the sun how dull and the fool how right and the beggar should be king for all the sense there is in life.

And say how nasty little creatures have no business lending hands. So they might come again and be cursed for the efforts.

And never leave.

Elf Trap

IT STARTED WITH RATS.

Out on the bird feeder. Graceful, leaping, acrobatic rodents, fawn-colored. Each rat performed a standing high jump from the pea gravel to the wild-bird feeder Norman had hung from the nectarine tree. The rats bulldozed the doves right off the feeder platform early each morning, and hunkered down to get fat on millet seed.

The jays put up a fight, yelling in bird language at the rats, but even a jay clears out when a rat airmails itself right into the middle of bird heaven, the feeder swinging back and forth.

At first I thought my eyes were mistaken, because my peepers aren't what they used to be. I take my sewing out in the early sun. I listen to the finches chirp and sing as I work on my quilts. Until recently they brought me no public acclaim. They are attractive combinations of calicos and ginghams and made-in-USA all-cotton fabrics you'll see on a calendar or my how-to book about quilting one of these days. I do my favorite sort of cooking in the morning, pig's feet and pork-leavings, the stuff butchers throw away. I make a tasty stew, and simmer it for hours while I sew.

"Rats!" I cried when I finally realized that the graceful, ravenous creatures were not some new bird life. "Norman, we've got rats bad!" My life has not been easy, my aching back requiring aspirin every night.

"I'll take care of them, Tina," he said.

Norman rescued cats from trees. He helped kids cross the street, holding up traffic. He looked after neighbor's gardens when they were on vacation. Everybody loved him. Norman was the one who would direct traffic every time the signal at Sixth and Cornell went out, which was often because of the brownouts.

The driving public loved him, and then when he did one of his Voices, the ones from the Disney series, drivers would ask him to sign an inflatable Wise Elf for the kids, or a Wise Elf action figure from Jack in the Box, which was hard because there was no real writing surface on the Wise Elf except across the face. Norman was the Elf-man in the eyes of the public, famous for creating the beloved elder elf for the movie, and the direct-to-video series, and then the CDs. Every time Hollywood needed an elf soundalike it was Norman's voice, until he got the polyp.

"I saved the day!" he would say, marching back to the house, accompanied by an Emeryville cop, congratulating him for being, once again, such a big help to the municipality. Norman would give the rookie man-in-blue a gnome, one of the concrete dwarves people put on lawns.

Or Norman would give a guest a big plastic Christmas elf that lit up if you popped a forty-watt all-weather bulb into the appropriate hole. Or a water nymph riding a dolphin, if his guest was highbrow, the dolphin being one of those half-fish, half-toad gargoyles the Renaissance artist favored instead of more naturalistic-looking water mammals. It was the nymph that mattered.

Norman was crazy about gremlins, dryads, pixies. He had

cuff links designed in Santa Fe, an elf's head, winking. That is, it was supposed to be a wink. The drawings looked like the elf-face copyrighted by the Disney Corporation, and borrowed by Norman who had, after all, made the Wise Elf a household name.

The cuff links, though, looked like gold-plated chewing gum, the sort you stick on the underside of theater seats, but it was the thought that counted. Elf neckties, elf monogrammed hankies, Wise Elf stationery, elf playing cards, elf-embossed Christmas greetings. Norman figured the elf was his totem, and that he was the elf's best friend on earth.

The trouble was that Norman actually believed in elves, and thought that when he got a check from his agent more or less on time it was the elves who had nudged the hairpiece-wearing saprophyte into taking the cap off his Montblanc.

Every time Norman remembered to take his umbrella out of a taxi or avoided stepping in some dog poop at the marina he'd boom, "Thank you, elves!" in a way if you didn't know him sounded cute. Norman believed the elves kept his roses from getting mildew, and kept whitefly off his Kentucky blue wonders.

He thought elves scurried around at night and tinkered with his pills. When the polyp shrank and didn't have to be surgically zapped, he believed it was because of elf effort. The surgeon said he'd never seen anything like it. Norman said, "It's the elves at work again." The surgeon chuckled, because who wouldn't, looking at a distinguished, robust, weathered but handsome man like Norman.

But Norman wasn't kidding. Every night he put out tiny brandy snifters he bought at a store that sold playhouse furnishings, four-star brandy, the best available, and when the liquor was partly evaporated the next morning he'd nod to me, and say, "What did I tell you?"

So when the rats came in battalions, more every morning, gymnastic, scrambling, circus rats, Norman frowned and said, "The elves'll lend a hand in this, Tina," like all we had to do was wait for the little guys to work up a military levy and march on the rats with drawn hat pins.

I suggested rat poison, and Norman said it made the animals suffer. I suggested a rat trap and he said maybe.

I had a plan that would cure Norman of elves, if I got up the nerve.

EVERYONE REMEMBERS the rat summer.

Rats owned the gardens, they owned the cellars, they danced in the dumpsters, they boogied down the fire escapes, they drove busses, they ran for public office. Very nearly. That was the summer that the rat was king, and desperate measures were required to eliminate a pest some said were our native California wood rat, denizen of hill and salt marsh, and not the chunky, bristly Norway rat at all. It made no difference to me. I nagged. I left Post-its on the fridge. No bird sang.

Norman bought a trap. A rat trap is exactly like a mousetrap, but bigger, cheap pinewood, with that wicked metal contraption, a spring and a hook. Norman baited it with a smudge of bacon fat, just as the man at the hardware store had suggested. I was pleased at Norman's efforts, but then I heard him talking out in the garden.

He was walking around the landscaping, talking to the lantana and the cherry tomato plants, saying, "Be careful of the trap — it's for rats." Norman stayed out there a long time, talking to the woodpile, talking to the bonsai maple, talking to every cranny in the garden, and even though I didn't have to ask, I did.

He said, "I'm warning the elves," like I was stupid to ask. People used to tell me I was lucky to be around such an elf-loving guy.

I told myself this was all the more reason to carry out my plan that very night.

THE NEXT MORNING neither one of us wanted to look. We don't like discovering dead things, even rats. We stalled, loading the dishwasher, listening to the short-wave, the local news from around the world, but at last Norman tiptoed out. He was gone a long time.

When he came back, he was ashen.

He couldn't say a word. "We got one," he said at last.

I said, "Terrific!" Although I myself was somewhat pale and shaken, I wasn't exactly surprised.

"No!" he said. "Tina, we got an elf!"

Sure enough, a crumpled body in a cute yellow jerkin and pointed shoes was half squashed under the business part of the trap. Worker ants were already dancing on the apparent corpse.

It was an elf-like cadaver, what you could make of it, although it didn't look like much, and Norman couldn't stand to do any sort of a postmortem. We buried the tiny interloper out by the ornamental lemon tree.

NORMAN'S COLLAPSE is well-known the world over.

How Disney security wouldn't let him on the lot in Burbank claiming they found some old memos of Norman's showing the famous late Mr. Walt D doing awful and awkward things to cartoon forest creatures. That would have passed over, but then one day when Norman was directing traffic he dragged a motorist from his Toyota for not coming to an immediate and complete stop.

Public opinion turned in a moment, and slogans were sprayed and banners were hung every night, accusing Norman of being a bully. Norman put out his little snifters, and every morning the rats had knocked over some, and left the others untouched.

Norman took to asking my opinion about things, which was a first – should we move to Ensenada, should he write an apology to the world. When my all-long-staple cotton quilt was selected by San Francisco's de Young Museum for inclusion in its Celebrate America jamboree, I was surprised and touched to hear Norman say, "I'm glad the elves remember one of us."

Things are much better now that Norman has almost totally stopped doing Wise Elf in the shower every morning, and stopped waiting for the phone to ring. I tell him to trim the star jasmine and put a redwood tree baby in the terra-cotta planter, and he does. I tell him to let the traffic pile up in the intersection, and he lets it. I give mail-order sewing lessons. I endorse a brand of thread.

This morning I had a tiny fire in the fireplace, burning tiny paper sewing patterns for a little jerkin and tiny shoes. And I burned up plans I had drawn, how to make a pig's ear into another shape entirely. I remember vividly how I never really made the thing – I cut the cloth, and got the needle and thread out on the kitchen sink, but my nerve failed.

It wasn't me. Some other hands did the work.

I came out that midnight for my aspirin and discovered a fake little dead man, all dressed up and ready for the trap. I put him out there in the trap with these two hands, telling myself I didn't hear the little footsteps and the tiny laughter.

I'm starting to believe it. I used to be the worst skeptic in the world, but not anymore.

For example, the bad thing that happened to Norman just last night, I didn't do that, either. The police came, and then the reporters gathered out by the curb, taking pictures of the house, with poor Norman in the hospital.

I couldn't be more upset that someone took a little needle and fine, silk thread, and stitched Norman's mouth shut.

Together Again

I HEARD THE CRY when it happened.

His Lordship's manservant came running to get me. The poor stripling was aghast, but I got up from polishing my cuirass, doing what any sergeant of the Horse Guard would be attending to on a Saturday afternoon, and I told him, "No worry, my dear young fellow, he's slipped and tumbled once or twice before now."

Slipped and fallen and let the town hear about it yelling, I did not add. What a stream of comment always flowed from our dear Mr. Dumpty. Lord Dumpty by then, of course, but those of us who knew him when, as they say, still had trouble reminding us that our very own Rotund One, as the ladies liked to call him, had become a life peer.

Day and night you'd hear Mr. Dumpty – Lord D, I mean – coming home from gaming or wine quaffing, giving his views on the weather and the speed of the carriage, whatever popped into his worthy mind. He was liberal with his opinions, was Lord Dumpty, and his voice was one that carried.

Lord D's voice was one of those forces of nature, you might say, and how such a force might be stopped was a subject of half-serious interest over many a tankard of ale. Indeed, that sunny

Saturday I could hear him even then, expostulating and ejaculating and even — I blush to add — blaspheming there where he had fallen, spurred into colorful verbal explosions by the pain of injury, as who could blame him.

And yet the very honor of serving His Lordship kept me confident as I mounted Old Gray, the charger good King George himself once stopped in front of just before Trafalgar and said, looking me in the eye, "Keep this one in oats, Mr. Hardwick!" That very horse.

Never mind I'm called Carrwitch, properly, and that no oat ever sprouted was good enough for the King's Horse Guard, man or beast. The poor king was in one of his rare collected humors, altogether himself that day, with his wig powdered and his stockings straight. That very horse was now eager to be off and to see what spirited adventure I had in mind for him that fore-Sabbath afternoon.

The shock of my life, it was.

Lord Dumpty had surmounted the Royal Terrace, that wall backed by the sweeping croquet lawn all the way up to St. James's, and perched up there, where he could comment favorably on the ladies, out loud, usually, and to their eternal blushes, for the most part. It wasn't the mounting of this venerable wall that posed the problem, as the bishop said to the maid, but it was the collision that followed when my lord mistook plain air for an extension of the royal grounds.

His Lordship had come a-cropper, and made a right mess of his new breeches.

In fashion breeches still were, trousers being seen only on Pall Mall, and only on the dandies and the ladies' men. Lord Dumpty was dignified, despite his habit of ceaseless speech, so he was in breeches and waistcoat, like any worthy of the House of Lords, and his well-cut draper's silk was all soiled with poor Lordship's eggy insides.

The poor gawky valet was close to tears. So I ordered the fellow — and I can give an order that straightens a gun in its carriage — to run off and muster the Horse Guard's surgeon. This was where the poor lad got his orders muddled, which was all my fault.

Written orders, as my own sergeant taught me, "Written and in-hand, please, Cardcastle," he'd say. In my early days it was all drill and look sharp, none of this dicing and smoking, each man his own tobacco. We all shared the same shag in my day, none of this each-man-his-own-pipe, or cigars handed around by the box. But without proper written orders the poor valet ran about alarming all the King's Horse that Lord Dumpty had fallen and was scattered from Shoreditch to Mayfair, not a moment to lose.

"What have we here?" said Furpin, the chief surgeon, squinting as he ran, entirely out of breath, with a jar of triple-star leeches under his arm.

In those days a surgeon would leech you, a barber would bleed you, and what with bedbugs and French lice, you'd be pale as a parson's nethers by the time you finished taking the day attending to your health. And even then it wasn't the surgeon's new Hessian boots or even his being without his spectacles that made it hard for him to offer Lord Dumpty something in the way of professional services. It was rock-solid incompetence that had Dr. Purblind crunch yet further portions of His Lordship under his heel.

All the same, Lord Dumpty was still on speaking terms with the world. He was entirely in his spirits, now that help seemed to have arrived, offering me the opinion that "I've slipped before, Sergeant Carefig, but never quite like this." He went on to compare this fall with other falls he'd taken, in divers places, with dates and times, to the best of his estimation. I had to agree that His Lordship had indeed slipped and indeed even fallen, but that this time he had won the toast.

But when the chief surgeon went head-over-heels on the noble yellow blood of his better, and further crushed the limb and girth of our Lord Dumpty, I knew that the arriving thunder of Horse Guard was worse than a bad idea. Never mind what they say about horse and men, I'll take a horse any day for good sense. Put a horse on a wall and see if he falls off, is what I say, in private, never one to criticize. And as for pandemonium, when a horse's courage fails him he runs off with his fellows, cheek to rump, and none of this jostling to get a good view.

I tried to halt the galloping guard, but they rode down upon us, despite me. By then, of course, Lord D was all hoof-and-yolk, and I had to employ my share of military language to set things right, and more than a few lads felt the bite of my riding crop later in the barracks. It was the fine crop with the brass plate near the handle, *in honor of Cajk Carwitch for his years of service,* from the men of the thirty-second of the King's Own Horse, since disbanded, I'm sorry to say, for drunkenness and general high jinks.

What service it required to gather His Lordship, you can only imagine.

Lord Dumpty's endless advice faded from quips to complaints to, once again, the sort of unfortunate language even our betters employ when patience is worn thin. The sight of the royal guard handling shoe and foot and rump and pate that had previously been attached to the selfsame congregated whole was enough to bring a tear to my own eye, I'm not ashamed to say.

THE STORY was told later, in all the taverns and inns of less-than-perfect repute, that all our men and all our horses — as though horses and men commingled much like flies on butter — could not put Lord Humphrey together again. Such calumny tries the patience of angels.

It is, of course, Lord Humphrey D, never Humpty — no man in my march would have dared whisper such a bastard version of His Lordship's Christian name. It was the Horse Guard, employed as one fine cooperative body after a bit of leather on my part, that plied the broken bits and spooned the poor, golden gore, and got His Lordship altogether into a loblolly's barrow, such as is used to carry amputated limbs so they don't distress the wounded by offering fresh evidence of their recent loss.

Thanks to the careful attendance of my own eye, if I must say so myself, and the shouldering aside of Chief Surgeon Forewind, whose eyesight had declined apace with his talent, Lord Dumpty was put together with a quart or two of apothecary's glue. Not that it was a pretty sight, and we kept Her Ladyship, Lord Dumpty's bride, out of the chamber as long as we could, until of course he was right sound again, with new breeches and a new waistcoat run up by his tailor, a Flemish gentleman whose name was all double o's and v's, and a papist into the bargain. And with a bucket or two of scooped-up yolk poured in, my lord was as good as ever before.

Very nearly.

There was, of course, the famous oversight. His Lordship was as right as a gentleman could be, and ready for the new trousers he would be wearing at the opera next season, run up by Van Overlook the tailor, or whatever the grinning foreigner's name was. Except, of course, search as all the lads might, no sign could be found of Lord Dumpty's most notorious and public part.

So that was where the libel began, the slur on the King's Horse Guard.

Never mind that the City was blessed and cheered by the sight for years to come of Lord H. Dumpty in high-waisted gabardine and top hat, boots and other such styles as never became him. And with barely a crack or chip to show where wall-sporting had been his downfall. They couldn't put him together, was the story that got about, even though only one thing was missing.

And if I keep among the brass plaques and inscriptions praising my steadfastness and even, if I may say so, my courage, an oddly shaped pink bibelot among my trophies, then how can I be anything but credited for winning my share of the king's peace?

I use it as a holder of cigar ash, now that this is the fashion, cheroots having supplanted the place of a pipe after beef, and I keep it ever at my elbow, or up on the table next to my pint of porter.

"What's that odd thing?" the visitor asks, and I let him hold it very gently, the eggshell mouth.

Arrival

[1]

"THERE ARE TWO DETECTIVES to see you, Mr. Eckman," said my receptionist, weary-hearted Lorna Quinn.

Her voice projected from the speaker box on my desk. I drummed my fingers on the blank legal pad in front of me and I thanked her.

This was very bad news, and I had every reason to panic, but I stayed right where I was.

I had very good reason to want to skitter down the fire escape, and out into the flow of happy-go-lucky men and women of San Francisco's financial district. The truth was, however, that while I was worried enough to run, I am not much of a runner, cursed with both a heavy build, and an equally hefty sense of shame.

I sat there feeling my future bleed out, my custom-tailored suit and handmade oxfords revealing themselves as the merest trappings of a man stripped to the bone by misfortune.

Lorna's voice did lift my mood just a tick, however, when her amplified voice added meaningfully, "They're looking for Mr. Adler."

I must have asked Lorna to send them in, because moments

later there they were, declining both coffee and diet Coke — two cops in plainclothes, looking capable of putting the handcuffs on me or on anyone else they might choose to take into custody.

"MY PARTNER Andy Adler is not here," I said with an air of formality as we all settled into our chairs, and before they could ask. I added, "And I have no idea where he is."

I smiled, a bleak grimace, I am sure, and the sort of don't-kick-me-when-I'm-down expression you aren't supposed to give anyone, let alone San Francisco police detectives. But I was beginning to hope that they were not really completely aware what a rat Andy Adler turned out to be, and how responsible I might be held for my partner's criminality. Besides, financial liability was not their concern. They were out to score successful arrests, and I was definitely not their man.

"Does he often disappear like this?" asked the female detective.

Detective Dee Glynn was quite an attractive woman, armed with a notebook that looked like a device designed for war. It was bristling with pen and pencil holders, a cell phone, a loop for holding earphones, and there was a set of loops for a small flashlight. The pen Detective Glynn was using, one of those see-through plastic Bics, was nearly out of ink, the blue-black depleted all the way down the shaft, and I got the impression she had used the ink up recently, writing down things seemingly innocent law partners had said about their crooked companions.

I kept my mouth shut for the time being and gave them another smile.

Andy had not disappeared — not in any literal, technical sense.

He had fled the country, I had to assume. Cheerful, likeable Andy had swapped his penthouse on Russian Hill for some plush hidey-hole in the Bahamas or Algiers — some avuncular police state with an anemic extradition treaty. He had fled with all our partnership's money, plush reserves owed to clients who had won recent lawsuits — thanks to my own skill at maneuvering and negotiating.

I was left owing money to a string of earnest and largely unwitting clients, with no means to pay it.

That's what happens in a law partnership when your partner rips off everyone he can for as much as he can rip. The hardworking, conscientious partner is left to cobble matters together, and face bankruptcy and a ravaged future if he fails. Thanks to Andy, my career was all but finished.

I was not taken downtown by the two cops. I had done nothing wrong personally. I even felt a look of pity creep over them, as they gave up their habitual distrust of lawyers to recognize me for what I was: an honest man who would never recover from this professional and financial meltdown.

"If he contacts you," said Detective Glynn, snapping and zipping her notebook, "you will call us."

This was a command, not a request.

"Andy is much too clever," I said, "to get in touch with me."

The detectives paused at the door. "How long," asked Detective Glynn, "have you known Mr. Adler?"

"We went to Hastings Law together," I said. "Played handball, took up fly fishing. We were friends."

"Not much of a friend, was he?" suggested Detective Glynn.

"I HAVE the molting mix for Mr. Le Grand," said Lorna as I buttoned my jacket, getting ready to leave for the evening.

Mr. Le Grand was my eighty-year-old Amazon parrot, handed down from my great uncle. He was a healthy bird, but his recent yearly molt made him drowsy and depressed. His *How do you like that?* — the sole remnant of my long-lost uncle's Philadelphia accent — came out thin and tired these days.

Lorna had dropped by a boutique pet shop near Union Square and bought this vitamin-rich bag of bird treats. Given my looming financial ruin, I wondered how long I would be able to employ this thoughtful woman, the sole support of her two gangly nine-year-old fraternal twins.

How long would I be able to keep all of this — my office, my license to practice law, everything I had worked for?

[2]

I USED TO take a cab home every night.

But it was time to begin pinching those precious pennies. I walked that evening — up Montgomery Street, across Broadway, and into North Beach, wondering if every shadowy tourist, every hurrying stockbroker, might be my partner, come back to make everything good. Never mind that I had, even then, the remains of a plushy existence, one any thinking person would envy.

At least, until he knew all the facts.

True, I had the fern-grotto apartment on Telegraph Hill. But it was a long, thin shotgun-style flat with a kitchen the size of my back pocket. The potted plants were evidence of my green thumb, but they also covered up the holes the landlord was too cheap to fix on the floor and in the just-post-1906 earthquake lath and plaster walls. The place smelled of a furtive, impossible to locate gas leak. The rooms were cruelly hot all September, and freezing throughout January.

I had an application in for the penthouse across the street, but the white-haired film director who lived there now was determined to endure there forever, and now I did not have enough to pay for so much as the first and last month's rent on such a beautiful place.

I drank the imported small-batch gin I bought at a breathtakingly high price, but the truth was that I was little more than an elegant pauper, all style but no wallet. I had long suspected that Andy Adler had been siphoning off more than his share of our cash flow.

Now I was sure.

I sorted through my banker's boxes of briefs, hoping that I had hard copy to contradict the strings of zeroes the office computer showed whenever I clicked on present accounts. I was not finding anything – except for a few odds and ends, the sort of items you locate in the bottom of a too-small closet.

One was a replica Colt .45, non-functional but gold-plated, presented to me by a grateful rancher for keeping his acreage out of the hands of an oil company. Another precious item was a bundle of love letters on cotton bond paper written in Waterman blue ink, all I had left of a love affair not ten months dead. Myrna Zeiss was a beauty, one of those women destined to pilot the world. I had, in the old-fashioned sense, courted her, and she had loved me in return, for a time.

Myrna had moved into an apartment in the Sunset with the underwater photographer Ted Pasqual, and when I ran into her on BART or at the art museum she gave me her thousand dollar smile but had no time for a cup of coffee.

One other important item of sentiment was a herm — a stone carving representing the god Hermes, purchased by me in Athens during a vacation a few years before, a soapstone replica of the plinths the ancient Greeks had positioned at major crossroads.

The utterance I made, hefting the curiosity in my hand, was not evidence of any religious inclination on my part, but it was heartfelt. I gave a wry little laugh, and said, "I sure wish some divinity could help me out of this mess."

I would reflect on that moment later, just as I recall it vividly now. A herm is an unusual and gently grotesque object, to modern eyes. A wise, philosophical-looking head is perched on a column with no suggestion of shoulders or torso. Halfway down the cylindrical column is a realistic set of male genitals, displayed as though thrust from within the stone, or as if the male reproductive organs fluttered about like butterflies, capable of alighting whither they would.

My choice of words, too, was a little strange. I said *divinity,* for example, and used a tone of sincere, if guarded, hopefulness. I am no more superstitious than any one else — I never read my horoscope, and crack open a fortune cookie expecting only to be amused. This was no ordinary crisis, however. I was not above asking for help from any quarter.

The souvenir from Athens's Plaka district had come with a small pamphlet, describing the god's attributes in French, English, and Greek. Hermes was messenger to Zeus, and the protector of travelers and businessmen, or any human activity that involved arrival. Hermes was, above all else, the god of tidings and approach. The sick called for his help because they awaited the arrival of good health, and the wanderer prayed for his own arrival, safe beside a cheery cooking fire.

"How do you like that?" Mr. Le Grand my distinguished parrot was saying, the pink and chartreuse bird treat all over his beak.

I had a cheddar cheese sandwich for dinner, washed down with the last of my expensive gin.

I WAS UP BEFORE DAWN the next morning, swallowing my cup of black stovetop espresso. My plan was running along the lines of how to avoid getting disbarred, and I was fairly certain that I myself would need a capable lawyer.

Mr. Le Grand gave me a chuckle, his typical greeting.

I walked to work, south along Montgomery Street.

The sun was slow, it seemed to me, to rise that day. Streetlights were still on, and although the traffic was already heavy, most cars still had their headlights blazing. I was brisk enough, giving my usual five dollar bill to the broken-down man with the dog-eared *Gulf Vet Blind and Crippled* sign. That meant that I would have to eat Kraft cheese and crackers for lunch, but I could stand to lose a pound or two.

I felt an odd lump, and a strange weight in the inside pocket of my sports jacket, and to my surprise I was carrying the soapstone herm to my office. I gave the idol a smile, feeling a little foolish and a little sad, a man whispering to a pagan souvenir.

As I crossed California Street I heard the huff, a sound not thunderous so much as vast and windy, as though a giant dictionary had slammed shut. The florist unloading her van in the predawn murk straightened from a bucket of princess lilies and said, "What was *that?*"

An explosion, a collision, I thought, or none of the above, just another random noise, perhaps a minor earthquake sending a garage door crashing. I whisked along through the lobby, took the elevator up ten floors, and I noted that Lorna was not yet at her desk.

I stopped outside my office, the key in my hand.

A shadow slipped along under the door, someone passing to and fro within. I considered the possibility that the janitorial service was at work, tidying my work space. This was very unlikely, however. I had called Sansome Street Janitorial the day before, explaining that we would not be needing their efficient but – I did not add – somewhat expensive services.

I knew that Andy must have slipped back into the office, pacing nervously, lies on his lips, and I braced myself. I did not want to set eyes on him. He had cheated, and deceived, and he had committed these sins against me, as well as his clients. My anger towards him was so keen that I had no clear idea of how to express it.

He was going to be suntanned and relaxed, and tell some sort of open-eyed untruth, how he had shoved the money into a Swiss bank under my name, and hand me a long series of slightly illegible photocopied numbers. I would pretend to believe him, and inwardly debate calling the police.

I am diffident and cautious, but in my way I face up to things in the end. I did not linger long in the hallway. I thrust the key in the slot, opened the door, and stepped into my office with as much dignity as I could muster.

I strode into my office, and said, "Good morning."

I put down my briefcase, arranged the folders on my desk, and put my hands on my hips in the sort of entrance a lawyer likes to make, cordial, no-nonsense, the sort of arrival that says I am taking charge.

To my surprise, however, I was speaking to an empty room.

[3]

THERE WAS NO ONE THERE.

A perfume surrounded me, a sweet, subtle scent, like the whiff of frankincense the visitor receives in a quiet church, but less cloying. The room was warm, too, pleasantly so – although the sun had yet to radiate through the windows with their view of the inky, early morning bay. There had not been enough daylight to throw a shadow under the door. I had been mistaken.

And yet I was not satisfied – not at all.

I felt in my marrow that I was not really alone.

Searching the room, I let the coat closet door swing open. It disclosed my trusty Burberry raincoat and Fox-frame umbrella, as well as a sheaf of blueprints left by a client who had sued the builder of his vacation home and agreed on a robust settlement – one of the clients who had just been robbed by Andy.

I looked into the lavatory attached to my office, and peered behind the wet bar. All of this made me realize ruefully that I was not going to be able to afford such a well-appointed office much longer.

It was then that a gentle, lively male voice startled me.

The tones were unfamiliar, and the accent was subtly foreign. The voice said, "Search no more, Peter Eckman."

A barely suppressed laugh suffused the words, and, unnerved, I glanced around the room.

My visitor was seated behind my desk, in the shadowy sanctuary of my high-backed leather chair – the one place where I would not have been able to discern him at once.

But I was certain that I had looked behind my desk on first

entering the room. Surely I had sat down for an instant in that very desk chair. Hadn't I put the briefcase down, right there, on the desktop?

So I greeted his remark with a surprised and slightly uneasy silence. He was still hard to make out as he sat there, a vague, slender individual in what looked like a pale, flowing mantle.

"Peter," he said, rising from the big chair, "Do you realize how long it has been since anyone sought my protection?"

I remained silent.

The word *protection* had a sinister, gangster-movie implication. I considered that he might be a particularly athletic burglar, or even a frightener — one of those thugs hired to intimidate and even injure. Or worse.

He might be a hit man. I was going to have any number of justifiably unhappy clients, and an actual hired killer, intent on shooting me dead, would not have been out of the question.

But even as I entertained these possibilities, I dismissed them. I was still uneasy, but I experienced none of the inner turmoil that danger quickens in the blood. Although I had been startled, I was not afraid of this unbidden guest, whoever he might prove to be.

I am sturdily built enough to step up to physical conflict, rather than flee it, but I recognized no particular menace in my visitor. I ransacked my supply of questions and commands, both courteous and blunt, but I could think of no way to either welcome him or to order him out of the office. Besides, I had the oddest sensation that we had met before.

And I was beginning — just beginning — to have that uncanny prickling hope, half joy, half terror, regarding the nature of the being I saw just then leaping from my chair and making his way across the room. He had a likeable air, vigorous and knowing, but soothing, too. As startling as I found him, he was the most agreeable person I had yet encountered in my life.

He perched on the bar with a boyish, athletic grace. "Check your accounts, Peter," he said with a smile. "Or do you desire to stand rooted to the carpet for the rest of the morning?"

"You've done something to the numbers, haven't you?" I asked — a cautious query, not giving way to hope just yet, but raising the prospect. This lad might be a computer wizard, a brilliant youth who could trick a balance sheet into showing whatever he chose.

He made a gesture, *Look and see.*

I turned on the computer and typed in my password: *Myrna Z.*

As I had guessed, where owlish zeroes had shown up the previous day, now my accounts were full of muscular numerals. My accounts looked like successfully completed math exams featuring large numbers and plenty of addition, higher sums than I had ever seen in my bank accounts before.

I took my time, closing down the computer, folding it, setting it safely on a corner of my desk. Awash in feeling, doubt alloyed with wishfulness, I stood and took a good look at my guest, stepping close to where he was sitting, swinging his legs.

He wore a light gray mantle, and a hood which was flung back to reveal a head of golden curls and a gray-eyed glance that was welcoming and all-knowing at once. I could not have guessed his age — his eyes were those of a veteran traveler, but his cheek and bearing were fresh, even childlike.

"But it's not real," I said. "A clever hacker can make the numbers vanish or show up, but there aren't any funds behind them. It's all fake."

He laughed. His was musical laughter, heart-healing. But it was laughter nonetheless, and I was a frayed professional disgusted by fraud and unwilling to be rescued by transparent trickery.

"Who asked you to fiddle my accounts?" I asked. And, I added, as though as an afterthought, "Who *are* you?"

It was not an afterthought at all. It was the essential question, although I was beginning to guess the answer.

"All is well, Peter," he said, bounding to the floor. "Your partner experienced a change of heart, reconstituted the funds, and provided you with some extra reserves he had tucked away. Your problems are over."

I straightened my cuffs and adjusted my tie, preparing to show this delightful presence just how efficiently our security guards can remove a trespasser from an office. But my heart wasn't in it. I was beginning to believe I knew who he was, and I was scared as well as excited.

"This is some sort of hoax," I said.

He laughed again, that wonderful, doubt-canceling music.

With a hurried knock, Lorna fluttered into the room with her coat still on. She gave no sign of seeing anyone in the room but me. Indeed, my visitor had vanished, and I was, as anyone could see, quite alone.

The sudden disappearance of my enigmatic visitor did not reassure me. Quite the contrary — I knew who he was beyond any question that moment, and I felt disengaged from reality.

"I heard you talking, Mr. Eckman," Lorna was saying, "and I was so relieved!"

I was able to speak, barely. "What's wrong?"

"I thought you might be dead!"

I had no quick response to that.

"You haven't heard?" she responded. "Oh my, you haven't heard at all. Please Mr. Eckman, you better sit down."

I sat.

"It was on KCBS," she said, "as I came up Van Ness Avenue." Lorna, like many good receptionists, has a talent for detail, but not necessarily a gift for brevity.

"What exactly," I asked her, "has happened?"

"They think it was a gas leak!" she exclaimed.

"Who?"

"The fire department — they're still putting out the blaze!"

"My apartment!"

"Your cute little place," she said, "with all the nice green houseplants? It blew up."

Mr. Le Grand! My beloved and distinguished bird, trapped in his cage, would not have had a chance in such an explosion.

"And your poor bird!" Lorna was saying.

[4]

I LEFT THE OFFICE, running as I have seen stunned people in disaster footage running, eyes open but only half-perceiving, rushing speechlessly.

I made haste across Broadway, toward Telegraph Hill where the smoke was rising and the fire department hoses were feathering water onto what was left of a handsome building.

My apartment had blown to so much confetti.

I recognized the odd items, my notepad from beside the kitchen phone, a dress shirt still in its slightly singed plastic covering, the way they come back from the laundry. But my home was gone, a gaping empty place where my plants and my bird had lived along with me.

Bits of spider plant and my favorite running shoes had blown all the way up the block. Strangers brought me fragments of my household, with warm-hearted, concerned expressions. "Is this yours, too?" they would ask, offering me the gold-plated revolver or a scrap of outdated legal document.

The blast had blown out windows throughout North Beach. There were no fatalities as yet, but the movie director was loaded into an ambulance — the explosion had caused him to collapse.

"Heart attack," confided a neighbor. "Looks pretty serious."

A photo hung on one heat blistered wall, exposed for the passing gawkers to see as the smoke subsided: Myrna Zeiss and I at the boardwalk in Santa Cruz, arm in arm, happy.

I RETURNED to my office by early afternoon, only to see Myrna sitting behind my desk, tearful and more beautiful than ever.

I had not seen her in months. We embraced.

"I am so glad, Peter," Myrna said, "so very happy that you aren't hurt. I couldn't bear it if something terrible happened to you, too."

"Me," I echoed, "too?"

"Ted has vanished," she said. "He was diving off Gorda, last week, getting photos of abalone fishing, and — "

She shrugged, looking desolate.

[5]

WHEN I WAS ALONE AGAIN, I withdrew the soapstone herm from my jacket pocket. I set it on the desk, beside my computer, and said, speaking fervently, "Divine Hermes, messenger of the Immortals, I thank you for your surprising bounty."

This much was true – along with freedom from financial and legal worries, the penthouse across the street was mine if I wanted it, and Myrna likewise could rejoin my life.

But in my tentative, diplomatic way, and despite my inexperience in dealing with the Immortals, I needed a degree of further consultation with the winged-with-awe, if he could spare me a few more moments of his attention.

"So Peter Eckman, you see," said the soul-quickening voice. "Your troubles have departed." He laughed, delighting in the great gifts he had bestowed upon an unworthy mortal.

"Indeed, Immortal Hermes, if I may so address you," I began, giving him something of a bow. "As you say, my troubles have – " I made a weary fluttering gesture with my hands. "I am grateful."

He bowed graciously in return, a likeable youth, and a source of light, if you saw him from the right angle.

"But I am brokenhearted as well," I said.

"How can this be, Peter?"

"Immortal one," I continued, "forgive me for being frank with you. How long has it been since you helped a human being?"

"Oh, centuries!" he answered with a smile. "Long centuries, Peter, since anyone has lifted a prayer to me."

"Is it possible, if you will forgive me," I went on, "that in your wisdom you have gotten rusty?"

His voice was just a little harsh, and his accent all the thicker when he said, "We Immortals experience no such decay, mortal supplicant."

My heart was so heavy that I was able to persist. "Perhaps, divine one, you are out of practice."

"Describe my failings, Peter Eckman."

His voice was cold.

Who was I to complain to an Immortal?

I made an effort to search for words.

At that moment a fluttering, green shape settled down against the window. There before the view of the bay, with tankers cutting wakes north toward the Richmond refineries, was Mr. Le Grand, his feathers awry and breathing hard.

I let out a glad cry.

"Surely you did not think," said Immortal Hermes, "that my gifts were endowed at the cost of irreconcilable suffering." His manner was stiff.

I let Mr. Le Grand into the room, and put him on the back of my chair. The bird chuckled happily.

"The underwater photographer has run off to Nice with his assistant," said the divinity with an air of hurt pride. "The film director will thrive in Palm Springs, with a new and nubile wife. Your apartment was going to explode within the month and take your life. I have healed it all."

Then he added, with something like a boy's petulance, "Shall I take your bounty away again?"

I was speechless with horror.

He laughed, clapping his hands, enjoying himself.

"Shall I ask Immortal Zeus to undo your blessings, Peter Eckman?"

I had nothing further to say, sure that to banter with a god was unimaginably foolish.

He stepped up to me, gave me the lightest, brotherly kiss on my lips. He passed through me, as sunlight lances a mist.

"More oranges," I heard him say, a musical voice in the distance.

I glanced around, feeling mortal, witless and ignorant.

"Mr. Le Grand," came the fading song, "should eat more citrus."

And he was gone.

Gravity

[1]

IT NEARLY COST ME MY LIFE, but at first I had little idea how dangerous my book about famous scientists could prove to be.

My twentieth book had received an award, Best Scientific Something of the Something, a newly created accolade that had never been given to any author before. Everyone wanted to read it, and I was awash in congratulatory messages. The book illuminated the private lives of famous scientists in a way that was kindhearted but not uncritical. The Einstein clan had sent me a thank you note, while the Oppenheimer heirs offered their "well done."

I was very busy. A publicist with an authoritative manner and a poor sense of geography wedged me into a three-week book tour from the gleaming malls of New Jersey to the book nooks of Santa Fe, every night a different venue. I kept myself smiling with those green pills I had bought in the hotel pharmacy in Mexico City the previous winter, and I was so elevated that I slept about forty-five minutes a night and lived on orange juice and peanuts, and not very many peanuts at that.

In a strip mall in San Diego, however, an anti-Darwinist tried to stab me to death, and he very nearly succeeded.

I had just arrived in my rented Jaguar four-door, accompanied by a security guard named Winston, a former deputy sheriff for San Bernardino County who was expert at eyeing exits and planning escape routes, should anything difficult take place. Winston was locating exit signs as I steered my way through a surprisingly energetic crowd of well-wishers, my Montblanc roller ball in hand. As I approached the unsubstantial-looking card table with its glossy stack of virgin volumes I became aware of an unsettling presence, not far away, over by the cookbooks.

He was bearded and garbed in a shapeless quilted jacket and a pair of outdoor, all-weather boots. He was tall but thin, and he made no effort to hide the large knife he withdrew as soon as I glanced his way, a prototypical Bowie knife with a dazzling and very long blade.

Even so, he had a meek, almost apologetic way about him, as though he wanted me to sign the carbon steel weapon with a Magic Marker, or admire its balance. Mack the Knife, I mentally tagged him. I expected him to step to the back of the line and wait his turn.

But he did have my attention.

Winston's gaze was drawn to this unsmiling individual, and the bulky former lawman began edging his way past the travel section, step by step seeking to interpose his body without causing undue alarm among the queuing shoppers.

Winston was too late.

Mack the K. was quick, eluding Winston's long arm. Mack performed a pirouette, as prettily as any NFL receiver, and when the knife entered my flesh I was aware that some long and very important moments had been cut out of the sequence of events.

Mack had reached me too quickly, as though a long strip of footage had been snipped from the archival celluloid. There he was, light of foot and quick of hand, but just slightly out of balance. Some hyperalert command center in my central nervous system had seen him coming.

I blocked him with my left arm, instinctively but effectively. The steel knifed my hip, a downward stroke that he must have envisioned severing my breastbone, cutting my heart in two. I was not hurt, I told myself, even as blood started down my Ermenegildo Zegna denims.

I wrestled Mack to the polished floor tiles. Winston picked him up and threw him against the wall, knocking down a display of crime novels.

I REPAIRED immediately to a local hospital, trundled there by an unnecessary but pleasingly dramatic ambulance, one of those red vans laden with oxygen tanks and featuring a very loud siren to go along with its flashing red and blue lights. I signed copies of my book for the paramedics on the way to the hospital, my autograph shaky and, I am afraid, almost impossible to read.

The ER doctor could not accept the possibility that a large knife had caused such a minor wound.

"You were very lucky," said the skeptical medico, convinced at last when police came to interview me.

Everyone left messages on the hotel phone, and I was up all night in my hotel room, the codeine wearing off and my spirits high. My old intimate friend and associate Eileen wondered if she should fly down from the Bay Area, but I said, feeling manly and invincible, that it was barely a nick.

But I was shaken.

The same command center in my nervous system that had preserved my life, now transmitted the knowledge that I had nearly lost that very life, and made me feel jumpy. When I read the *San Diego Union*'s account of the assault, and the pamphlets found in my assailant's multitude of ample, zippered jacket pockets, I had to put the newspaper away.

"Darwin Hoax Threat to Constitution," declared one of the booklets. "Science Akin to Devil Worship" was another title. The knife-wielding Roland Boone was an aspiring author, and the bookstore had refused to sell his pamphlets.

THE SHOW, of course, had to go on, and I continued my book tour.

The publisher provided two new security people, a man and a woman, and I was reassured by them. Superficially I was confident, a spring in my only slightly limping step. My wound was healing nicely, and needed only a large Band-aid to cover the little smile on my hip. There would not be much of a scar.

But I was looking forward to going home. I was weary, and I was hungry for solitude.

Home was, however, the very place I would not be able to go.

As my tour was winding down and I signed title pages of *Naked Science* in mega-complexes in Portland and Seattle, back in my place of permanent residence all was not well. A Union Pacific freight train derailed beside my high-rise condominium complex in the East Bay, dioxin and an unnamed yellowish powder closing off a mile of Interstate Eighty. A ten-acre area of

Berkeley and Albany was closed off by the fire department and Homeland Security. As I sat the day after my last signing beside Seattle's Lake Washington, I had no home to safely and legally steal back to.

I was ready to lie down for a week or two, and I was beginning to wonder if perhaps a steady diet of Benzedrine and monkey thyroid – if that is what it was – provided the most reliable footing for a healthy way of life. My clothes hung on me, several sizes too big.

I had decided that morning that the face I saw staring back at me from the bathroom mirror was a haggard stranger, and I put the remaining vial of power-tablets in my shaving kit and zipped it shut. I unpeeled the plastic canopy over the hotel's Healthy Choice fruit basket, an unnaturally ruddy apple beside a waxy-looking navel orange, a firm yellow banana, and a blueberry muffin wrapped in its own, close-fitting plastic covering.

I was about to begin my path toward better nutrition – if not life itself – when the phone rang, and it was my old friend again, Eileen Threllkill of the National Academy of Science.

"How is your injury?" asked Eileen.

"Healing handsomely."

"Are you sure?" she inquired. "You sound a little shaky."

"I haven't eaten breakfast," I said in response.

In about three weeks, I did not add.

Eileen was one of my favorite contacts in the world of science, an Oxford woman with a reputation for knowing everything and everyone. We had coauthored an article a few years back describing the strong possibility that Michelangelo carved counterfeit Greek statues to give the academics of his day something to get excited about, and Eileen and I gave tone to panels around the globe on subjects like scientific ethics, global warming, and the art of biography.

I was known for my gift of understanding my subjects — how they spoke, what they loved, what their lives had been like. "If any modern journalist," said one of my generous colleagues at the London *Times*, "could sit down and have a pint with Galileo and make him feel at home, it would be Milton Collins."

"I can't say very much on the phone," said Eileen. "This is all extremely hush-hush."

Her excited tone, compressing her voice to a stage whisper, had me sitting straight, alive with curiosity. "Eileen, give me a hint."

"You and I are due in London tomorrow," she said. "Something very big has happened, Milton, and they want us in on it."

"'They?'"

"This is huge, Milton. It may be the single most remarkable scientific event of the last four hundred years."

I blinked, trying to think of an appropriate response.

"It has been a fairly busy four centuries, Eileen," I responded cautiously. "Maybe you're just a wee bit carried away." Eileen's enthusiasm and excitement were contagious — as always — but I did not relish a ten-hour flight to Heathrow.

"Let me just give you that hint you wanted, Milton," she said, "in the form of a famous equation."

She was so quietly excited that she had to stop talking for a moment. When she spoke again she uttered the formula, "$F=ma$," in a tone that meant: this will explain everything.

She paused, as though that Newtonian chestnut would be enough to send me racing to the airport.

If Eileen has a failing – and I like her very much, and have sometimes wondered why we aren't man and wife – it is that she has a better head for numbers and abstractions than I do. She becomes impatient when I don't immediately understand some abstruse allusion.

I prefer sentences with nouns and verbs to equations, and I was just a little testy that morning. "The British government has discovered that when you push something it moves?"

"No, Milton," said Eileen, in an excited whisper that the phone amplified like a whip crack. "They have him – they have brought him back."

I was still deeply puzzled. "Who?"

"The very man himself!"

[2]

I DID NOT SLEEP during the flight.

Eileen was waiting for me at Heathrow, along with a security guard.

My friend had arrived forty-five minutes ahead of me from San Francisco, but she could have been in London for weeks. Her red hair was gathered into a tiny bun, her sweater was unwrinkled and her pretty, welcome smile just the thing I needed to see.

I was wearing a pair of Tony Lama boots, denims, and a Harris tweed coat, my usual travel wear – and the clothes I tend to wear to meetings and social occasions, too. My clothes were not cheap – but they were thoroughly rumpled.

"Good heavens, Milton," said Eileen, sizing me up. "You look like a living corpse."

"Thanks, Eileen."

"Are you sure your wound isn't bothering you?"

"I am as fit as I ever was," I insisted.

She murmured into my ear, conspiratorially, "You want to make the right impression on Lord M."

"Who?"

"Harold Hare, Lord Muchly, Her Majesty's government favorite fifty-year-old whiz kid. He was a little doubtful that you would be able to help. I pushed for you with 'Milton's just your man,' and now you show up looking like a rat's ghost."

I stepped over to a men's room. I washed my gaunt but still residually decent looking visage, combed my hair and choked down one of my Mexican Refreshers, and at once began to feel better.

But despite my best efforts I still did not look very good. Incipient jaundice was creeping into the whites of my eyes, and my lips were so chapped they appeared desiccated. My wound, which had not been hurting, was smarting now after the long flight, a nagging reminder that I had nearly lost my life.

Eileen took my hand as we faced the brazen sunlight beyond the terminal exit. "It is so good to see you, Milton," she said. She gave my hand a squeeze. "What's left of you."

THE SECURITY GUARD, with a radio receiver stuck into his left ear like a hearing aid, drove an airtight, dark blue Rover from the airport as Eileen leaned toward me and said, "We can talk."

"Seattle was very pretty," I said, keeping to safe subjects for my own sanity's sake. "Sunny – not a drop of rain."

"You will want to know," said Eileen, with her gift for ignoring small talk, "how a human being who died in 1727 from old age and mercury poisoning can be brought back to life."

Isaac Newton had described gravity, discovered the laws of

motion, created calculus, and served in Parliament. He spent the last decades of his life studying alchemy, and the use of mercury in separating gold from dross, among other procedures, was believed to have had no beneficial effect on his health.

"That's what I would like to know, yes," I agreed diffidently.

My curiosity and wonderment were alloyed with deepest skepticism, and I suspected a prank of some sort – a rank hoax.

"The mercury preserved him, oddly enough," said Eileen.

That did sound odd, but I said nothing as Eileen described experiments over the years, using mercury solvents as a preservative in processes unrelated to bringing any famous mind back into existence. Thimerosal and other preparations were mentioned, preserving flu vaccines and saline solution for contact lenses, and then Eileen's techno-vocabulary outstripped my ability to follow her.

Her briefing had something to do with the inevitable electrical current, the corpse really in very nearly mint condition what with being positively blue with mercury, a little tweaking of the brain chemistry and the ambitious neurosurgeon named Harold Hare, a life peer and "the wizard behind all this."

I have never spent much time in Kensington or Mayfair, finding that Bloomsbury and the British Museum gave me the research facilities I needed while I adjusted to new time zones and fine-tuned my packing for Moscow or Tel Aviv. The impression I had, as we sped past the Natural Science Museum, was that London was celebrating the month of May on a scale I had never observed in any city before.

The plane trees of Hyde Park were in full leaf, and shoppers and joggers, taxis and lorries all purred along as though already in on the secret that death had, indeed, no reason to be proud.

"But they tell me there are some problems," Eileen murmured confidingly.

"I'm not surprised," I said.

We pulled up into a gated, side entrance to an anonymous modern building sporting the sign *H. M. Export and Design Centre*, a name calculated to give rise to inconvenient curiosity in no one.

"After great initial joy, Lord M. confides to me," Eileen went on, "things have started to go wrong."

A gate opened, a woman in a blue uniform looked at the three of us, wrote down our names with elaborate care, and then the Rover descended into the shadowy car park secured under the bland but highly secure fortress.

"THE TWO OF YOU AT LAST, and I am afraid both running rather late."

This was said all in a rush by a man whose smile was an expression of brisk unhappiness.

Eileen offered an introduction, but his lordship waved it aside as though courtesy was cumbersome. He put his hand on my shoulder, both gentle and peremptory, silencing my questions before I could start.

"Mr. Collins," he said, peering into my eyes, "I shall talk, and you will listen."

"Anything I can do," I said.

The man was the picture of authoritarian science, his long white lab coat fluttering, and his pockets bulging an assortment of digital devices. As we followed Lord Muchly, he tugged a surgical cap over his shiny head, a translucent, cartilage-gray shower cap. An assistant, a slender, dark-haired young woman, handed

Eileen and me each packages containing several pounds of protective plastic garb, and blue, disposable breathing masks.

"What you can do," Harold said, stopping before a stainless steel door, "is make our distinguished personage feel just a little more gratitude." He tugged plastic booties over his shoes, and indicated that we were to do the same.

"How?" asked Eileen.

"By helping him to understand that we brought him back to existence to improve our lives," said Lord M. "We need a top mind at work on solving such a host of problems." He turned and gave us a critical smile. He gave me an additional, searching glance. "Are you well?" he asked.

"Quite," I said. "Entirely." I was feeling light-headed, however, even a little faint.

The stainless steel door hissed shut behind us.

"Our government has not brought Sir Isaac back to be a living marvel," he said. "Although we expect your book, when you write it, and the subsequent licensing of films and Sir Isaac action figures and dolls and such, will bring in a good deal on the cash side of the ledger."

Our steps made squishy, squeaky sounds in our unfamiliar footwear as we hurried along yet another corridor. We reached a further door, painted medicine cabinet white. The air here smelled of sterility, ozone, and antiseptics, and the lights, while bright, were the science fiction lavender shade I associated with ultraviolet tanning cubicles.

"We need him to help us," said Lord M. "New sources of energy, new defense technology. Think what the old wise head can do for you and me, if and when it gets around to working as it should."

The distinguished man of science adjusted the elastic band around his head. And then reached for a speaker box beside the forbidding white door. He turned a volume dial, and one of those static-ridden, electrical silences ensued, as non-communicative as distant rainfall.

Then I heard it, quite clearly.

A very feeble, stricken sounding voice was lifted in sorrow.

Someone beyond the impervious white door was weeping.

Harold turned off the sound and shook his head with a sigh. The motion made his shower cap wrinkle and unwrinkle, with an insistent if subtle noise, as though his head was swelling and contracting. I had never before realized how inhuman such caps make us look.

Tears flooded my eyes, involuntarily, at the sound of such deeply heartfelt grief.

"Sir Isaac has inferred what has happened," said Lord Muchly, all the starch absent from his voice. "He knew we had brought him back to life as soon as I stepped into the room and introduced myself."

"How could he guess?" asked Eileen.

"This is one of the most intelligent human beings who ever drew a breath, Eileen," said Lord M. "Do you think we could deceive him for an instant? 'Sir, you are not of age in which I lived,' he said to me. 'I have died, suffered to be revitalized into a solitary prison, and you are my chief keeper.'"

"How dreadful!" she said.

"And then," said Lord M., "Sir Isaac began to weep."

"What can we do?" asked Eileen.

"He has wept for three days," said Lord M. "He sleeps only to reawaken and begin his mourning all over again."

"Mourning?" asked Eileen.

"How else could the poor fellow feel," I interjected. "He knows all the people he loved must be long dead, and I don't think his Lord Muchly's appearance is quite reassuring, either."

For the first time Lord Muchly looked at me with something like surprised respect. "You mean, my protective garb may have put him off?"

"You should have gone to one of those barrister supply shops," I suggested. "Or Angel's, the theatrical costumers. A horsehair wig and a judge's robe would have looked gentlemanly to someone of Sir Isaac's background."

Lord Muchly made an affirmative "Mmm," his lips pressed together thoughtfully. "It is too late to correct an unfortunate first impression, I'm afraid."

"And your speech was probably too modern as well," I went on. "You need to dip into Swift and Dryden, brush up on your early eighteenth-century word power. You probably told him he'd need a CAT scan or an MRI or said his white cell count was low. Newton never knew what a germ was, let alone a lightbulb."

"You make a good point," said Lord M. "But as I have said – I cannot undo an awkward first impression."

"But he hasn't yet met Milton," said Eileen.

Up to that moment I had been carried along by what I had foreseen as my marginal participation in this bright episode in scientific history. The sound of the ghostly, ancient voice raised in ceaseless sorrow, however, had shaken my spirits more than I was willing to admit, even to myself. I was not ready to set eyes on this living relic, and I certainly was unprepared to confront whatever was left, after all these years, of the founder of modern thought.

I wanted to be far away, in a peaceful, fertile landscape, among leafy shrubs and lowing cattle, although at that point any version of the outdoors would have sufficed.

I was in no mood to meet a living corpse, and I must have said something to that effect. At that precise moment I lost an instant of time, painlessly but utterly.

The next thing I knew, I was sitting, suddenly unexpectedly, with my back against a wall. I realized that I must have fainted.

"I'm sorry you're not feeling well," said Eileen, kneeling beside me. "I knew you didn't look the picture of vitality."

"What could be better?" I asked, despite my profound misgivings. "If I look half dead I should be perfect for the job."

"It's a pity you won't be much use to us, Mr. Collins," sighed Lord M.

"Send me in to meet Sir Isaac!" I said.

I wished I had never met that suave, Danish-born pharmacist in that plush, Zona Rosa hotel. "Two a day, and life will be OK," he had promised, speaking American English as though it was a form of nursery rhyme.

I had asked what they were and he had made a side-to-side motion of his hand. I had found it funny, his *a little of this, a little of that* gesture. I had gone so far as to laugh. The last three weeks had been a colorful blur, but it grimly occurred to me now that as easy as life felt, death seemed that much easier.

"Mr. Collins," said Lord M., "you are unable to so much as stand up."

He uttered the last two words with special emphasis, loading the words with such anticipated disappointment and knowing exasperation, that I was able to climb shakily to my feet, prompted by professional pride as much as anything else.

"I feel like a dead man," I said, with something like happiness coloring my voice.

"And I am afraid you look very much the part," said his lordship.

"I feel like a corpse, and I can remember just enough of 'A Modest Proposal' and other such works to speak the appropriate tongue. Get me a wheelchair," I added, "and speed me in to see our very, very late scientist. Quickly, before I change my mind."

[3]

I DON'T KNOW WHAT I HAD EXPECTED.

But if I piece together the vague images I had in mind before I was rolled into the Vitrification Chamber they would have been languorous fantasies, composed of half-remembered watercolors of sickrooms, wounded soldiers recovering in drawing rooms, tubercular curates enjoying the cheery hearth.

I knew so little about what Sir Isaac might have undergone, that my store of fantasies, once I set aside lurid melodramas featuring mad scientists on the one hand, and Victorian artwork featuring sickly poets on the other, was a desert populated with the most ignorant and sentimental motifs.

Lord M. was grateful, once I convinced him of the soundness of my plan. He remained prickly and hard to please, but once again I sensed a tone of respect seep into his manner. Eileen was much more quiet. I was undertaking something grave, and she knew it. She lacked that masculine ability to frog-march her bleak spirits onto sunnier and optimistic grounds. Once she felt a plan was unwise, no amount of pep talk could persuade her otherwise.

"It won't work," was all she would offer by way of protest,

and she kept repeating herself.

As soon as the key went into the lock of the blank, white barrier the weeping stopped.

Someone – some very important, stricken once and future human being – was listening.

Lord M. opened the heavy, white doors, and a gust of warm air hit me, as warm and scented with filth as any superheated poultry house. I had a vivid impression of a dark hall, and an equally dark room, with a pool of very bright light in one corner, the illumination thrown down on a hospital bed occupied by a pile of blue rags.

The slim attendant, with strong arms and a steady stride, wheeled me into the dark, and then she left me. The key rattled, a pressure lock hissed, and the door was sealed behind me.

I was alone in the warm darkness.

Or perhaps not entirely alone.

The odor in the room was of the grave, the charnel house, of decay thwarted but not conquered. I hated the smell.

I became aware of being watched. To my horror, when I glanced – against my better judgment – toward the tattered inky blue scraps on the white sheets of the bed I saw a pair of eyes.

A pair of dark pupils set in blue-gray irises.

Now that they had my attention, I could not look away.

A pair of eyes was looking at me intently, from the depths of a hooded mantle, the sort of warm-up robe I associate with athletes, boxers, and gymnasts.

I had a half-formed introduction ready, mentally rehearsed over the hasty minutes of our preparation. Formal, appropriate speech was poised on my tongue delineating how distressed

I, too, felt at having been disgorged from a grave. I knew my part in this dramatic fiction well.

I was a fellow dead man brought back from some point in the twentieth century – I had picked my father's birth date. And I was ready to complain about Lord Muchly, and wonder what would become of any mortal lucky or unlucky enough to be plucked from the tomb. I had the language in pretty good order, unmodern modern English, King James Bible diction mixed with a little Dryden.

A camera in each corner of the room spied on us. I was aware that Muchly and Eileen must be sitting outside the door, listening.

I was ready.

But I changed my mind.

Instead, bypassing all my self-scripted conversational gambit, I said, "Please accept my apologies, Sir Isaac."

He said nothing in response – if indeed that tangle of remnant cloth was our celebrated guest.

"On behalf of my own era, my colleagues, and my world – I apologize. You did not seek this," I continued, "and here you are."

I got up, able to stand quite comfortably now that my lightheadedness had passed. I rolled the wheelchair into a corner of the room. "I was going to pretend to be a dead man revitalized, just like you. But then it didn't seem right."

There was a silence.

And the sound of his breathing.

The silence remained unbroken by speech.

Then, "What manner of man are you, sir?" came the hoarse query.

The words were just understandable, through an accent that sounded like a nearly comical caricature of obscure British regional dialect, upper-crust and nasal, rural and rasping all at once. One corner of my mind had remained doubtful, but now that doubt vanished.

Not even an ingenious hoax could devise such an accent, or such a searching, plaintive voice.

"My name is Milton Collins," I said, speaking slowly and with heartfelt respect, realizing how quack-quack my Americana diction must sound.

"Are you, sir, a Dutchman?"

The question made me stop. I was thrilled, but I felt cautious, too. "No, sir, I am not."

He did not respond for a long moment.

Then he asked, "Are you, sir, any manner of Irishman, perhaps?"

"I am not an Irishman, Sir Isaac."

Then he added, "I hope, sir, my question has not offended you. My spirits are low, my judgment is perhaps unsound."

"Not at all," I said at once.

I was kindled by the course of this conversation, lifted into unusual if not unnatural courtesy and gentleness by his particular manner. More than anything, I wished to do no harm.

"Your servant is ill-mannered," came the proud, feeble accents, "if you will forgive me for observing."

"My servant?"

"That man in the long white livery and the strange cap."

"I am sorry he has offended you."

"Your man — what is his name?"

"Muchly."

"Is he quite – " He enunciated a string of Latin words, and only through luck and a long memory was I able to catch the drift.

He was asking, in crisp Latin, if Lord M. was of healthy mind. I lifted my hand. "My memory of the Roman language is faulty, sir, but I can assure you Muchly is harmless. But proud – to the point of vanity."

It was then that Sir Isaac sat up, and the hood fell from his head. "He articulates the assertion that he has arrived from Heaven – as well as I can understand his meaning – to trouble my peace."

The man was as blue as any victim of mercury poisoning, and bald, and withered. He looked every bit the man now older than centuries, and yet, as he ran a blue gray tongue over his lips, and reached his claw-like hands under the coverlets, he did look like a man returned to life and possessed of his wits.

"You understand, Sir Isaac," I said, speaking with a ginger earnestness, "that you are alive hundreds of years after you closed your eyes."

"I am dead."

"You are alive, Sir Isaac, after having died," I said.

Was that a twinkle I saw in his eye? "So your man tried to make me believe. And I have grieved, feeling the loss of so much."

"Sir Isaac, I hope your sorrow can end."

"Perhaps," he suggested hopefully, "my spirits will lift through the administration of some physic."

Having come so far I had to continue. "How is it," I asked, "that you recognize Muchly as servant, and see me as his master?"

"Am I mistaken, sir?"

"Sir Isaac, I am not a man to argue with a philosopher as learned and well-regarded as yourself."

"You've been out hunting," said the scientist, "as I judge by your clothes, your boots, your rude but well-knit tweeds taken altogether. Further, if you will forgive my saying so, you have the rough manner and round ignorance of speech of a man of property and name. And you speak with a wooden discourtesy, as only an aristocrat would choose to do."

If I was offended, I made no sound.

"While your man – Muchly, with his officious and bristling way. Anyone could see what a niggling amanuensis he must be, calling attention to his many accomplishments."

"Be merciful to him, if you will," I said. "Which of us is without fault? Be kindhearted toward all of us, Sir Isaac."

"If my spirits could be uplifted, my lord," he said, "by any means, I would be well pleased."

I felt in my pocket the weight of the Mexican pills. Perhaps a half – or a tenth of a half – of one of my mystery tablets would brush away his melancholy. The drug might, at the same time, rupture a cardiovascular system that was doing well to let him sit up and talk.

Shouldn't I, I wondered, let the discoverer of the laws of motion make the decision himself? Or would such an experiment only prove disastrous?

"This preparation might well answer," I said. "Or – perhaps it might not."

"What variety of preparation," he asked hopefully, "are you offering me?"

I selected a tablet, held it forth, and his mummified-looking, blue hand closed around it.

"Like any medicine," I said, "this might well be thought a poison."

"At last," said Sir Isaac, "someone is willing and able to use me well."

"There may be more than a little danger involved, Sir Isaac. The risk may be too great."

"Have you partaken," asked Sir Isaac, "of this medication yourself?"

A fluttering sound came from outside. Muchly pounding on the speaker, no doubt, or hurrying toward the door, trying to wrestle it open. I sensed their horror that I was about to offer Sir Isaac some unexamined substance.

"Indeed I have."

He eyed me for signs of health or morbidity.

"We must make our future known, my friend," Sir Isaac said at last, "through experimentation."

[4]

IT RAINS, and then the rain stops. The sky opens, and the sunlight is like the first sun, ever.

From where we live I can see a river, and a distant green slope. In the summer the upward rising acres ripen into solemn bronze. They are hayfields, and after cutting the rolls of hay dot the distance, waiting sometimes for weeks before field hands arrive to finish gathering the harvest.

The moon rises over hills and you see how the world waits to be seen — observed and at least partly understood. And how before the mind lifted to wonder at it all the void of our multi-colored earth was all but empty.

I can also just make out the security teams from the terrace. Armed with automatic rifles, secretive but still visible, sentries ensure that no wanderer approaches our safe refuge. We can leave for a stroll among the hedgerows if we choose, or we can drowse beside one of the glorious fireplaces.

We have everything we want. When the brandy is esteemed not nearly old enough, barrels of the century-old cognac are secured, and manhandled into the wine cellar with apologies from the staff. When we desire new artworks on the walls, a Rubens cartoon, or a Rembrandt self-portrait, curators from the National Gallery consult with us, offering the best that can be eagerly loaned to us from museums around the globe.

The entire world holds nothing back in its generosity. No carpet is too rare, no fruit out-of-season. When I sleep I am all the more grateful to be alive now. Life is short, I know, even when it is not.

Sir Isaac calls me the one man he can trust, although he grows increasingly fond of Eileen. I write up my experiences, and every day is a new wonder.

"Explain how," he asks, "the loom works, the one that weaves my new breeches."

"I can't," I tell him, for the hundredth – the thousandth – time. I don't know very much about how anything works, and he finds this both frustrating and amusing. He undertakes to theorize how he thinks my pen, my watch, my telephone work – and he is probably right.

He laughs affectionately, and calls me his ignorant lord, the man appointed his guardian and companion, while scientists and dignitaries queue at the bottom of the garden, pilgrims seeking an audience. Even Lord M. has to wait his turn, and Eileen helps me schedule appointments, fussily declining film stars, diplomats, heads of state.

WE RELISH our solitude.